First edition independently printed 2023.
This edition printed 2024 by Pope Lick Press.

DEREK HEATH

NIGHT OF THE BUNNY

POPE LICK PRESS

2024

PART ONE

HUNT

1

Fire boiled through the office, rippling across a streak of oily silver on the carpet and clawing hungrily at the corners of an old pine desk. One of the curtains had caught and the narrow windows behind its billowing, blackening husk swelled with flickering amber pools.

'Find him!' Mother Brunheldt yelled over the crackling and the shriek of the alarm, bundling the unlit curtain into her arms and swaddling the flaming mess of the other with it, smacking fabric into fabric in a desperate effort to quench the fire. Behind her an explosion of white powder consumed the desk as one of the sisters compressed the trigger of a battered extinguisher, spraying the base of the fire with gritted teeth. An ember sizzled through the nun's habit and she yowled, letting go of the extinguisher's hose to bat at the tiny yellow spark. Mother Brunheldt had finished with the curtains and she snatched the extinguisher, punching a generous dose of white powder into the carpet. '*Find him!*'

Sister Emmanuel hurried out of the room, rosary rattling at her waist as she clutched the hem of her gown with both hands. Brunheldt had sent the rest of them after him, too, and she could hear yelling from one of the classrooms on the floor below. She stamped out the last wet tongues of the fire whimpering at her feet and paused for breath, staring dismayed at the black shredded network of fibres that remained of the curtains.

'Oh, you little fucker,' the old woman snarled through her teeth, her voice lost beneath the continued scream of the piping fire alarm. She wiped sweat from her wrinkled throat and cheeks and moved past the desk, despairing over the charred papers scattered about it on the floor. Little mounds of powder sat, browned like burnt meringue, around the legs of the desk and a little drift of the stuff decorated its surface. The wood was marked through with patches of pitch-black. The whole office smelled of smoke and burning plastic. Mother Brunheldt reached up for the latch of the window and shoved it open, coughing into one hand as she swiped the air with the other.

Below, the playground of St. Adjutor's Academy was flooded with a squabble of frantic kids, some filed half-neatly in their muster rows but most stood in haphazard clumps and gawped up at the office window, hands raised to their brows to blot out the sun. A thin pillar of smoke billowed from one of the lower windows of the building and spilled across the tarmac like mist; she trusted, from the lack of confused screaming, that the fire in the caretaker's break room had also been put out. In one corner of the playground the swimming team stood hopping about in their kits, huddled together as though that might save their modesty. Poor blighters hadn't stopped for towels; good on them for following procedure, she supposed, but she was moderately embarrassed to see that none of the other kids had offered any of the half-naked swimmers a jacket or coat.

The fire alarm died suddenly, an eerie silence falling upon the scene outside. A bedraggled knot of teachers and nuns separated and began shepherding the kids into their rows, a stern-looking sister handing out clipboards. Mother Brunheldt let out her breath, her fists finally loosening as her heartbeat began to return to its normal tempo.

Behind her, clipped heels rang loudly on the floorboards in the hallway, growing louder as they approached the office. 'Here we go,' she murmured sourly, turning to face the open door.

Two of the sisters paraded the boy into the room and threw him forward, his shoes scuffing the carpet. The nuns stepped back, standing at attention either side of the door like stern-faced sentinels.

'Is everybody out of the building?' Bunheldt said quietly, ignoring the boy for now. The abashed sixteen-year-old stood in the middle of the room, scruffy in his shirt and tie, sleeves rolled up to reveal forearms crisscrossed with yellowing bruises. His head was bowed, face hidden beneath a mop of scruffy sandy hair. There was something square and silver in his fist.

'Yes,' Sister Paton nodded briskly, sunlight glinting off the cross hanging against her chest. 'All the kids, we believe. Sisters Ling and Ridgers are conducting one last search.'

Brunheldt nodded. Looking down at the boy as she moved to her scorched desk, she asked, 'Anybody *hurt*?'

'Not that we know of,' Sister Paton said.

'The caretaker was at the other end of the building when the fire broke out in his break room,' said the other nun, 'minimal damage. We may need to replace his chair.'

'His chair. My desk; my curtains,' Brunheldt nodded. She spoke sharply in the child's direction: 'Starts adding up, doesn't it, boy?'

The boy said nothing, his head low, hands hanging at his sides. His whole body seemed to be trembling, she noted. Not fear, though; he was angry at being caught, she supposed.

'That'll be all,' she said quietly.

Sisters Paton and Sedgwick glanced at each other. 'Are you sure?' Paton said. 'Wouldn't you like us to—'

'That'll be all,' Brunheldt repeated, smiling thinly at them. The sisters nodded politely before turning to step out of the door. Sedgwick closed it behind them with a soft *click*, casting one last hateful look in the boy's direction before they disappeared, footsteps retreating down the hall.

Mother Brunheldt turned back to the boy.

'What do you have to say for yourself?'

He looked up, green eyes flashing angrily beneath the mess of his fringe. More bruises spattered the soft flesh of his neck, just above the collar, pale with age but still defined enough to betray the shapes of thin, squeezing fingers.

Brunheldt swallowed. 'Nothing, eh?'

The boy's jaw was clenched hard, his face a knot of quiet fury. Almost casually, he stuffed his hands into the pockets of his shorts, tucking away the lighter before it could be confiscated. Well, she had higher aspirations than that.

'Two fires at once,' she said calmly, her tone almost admiring. 'You know we can't tolerate this.'

The boy shrugged. There was a spatter of gasoline on his polished black shoe, she noticed.

Brunheldt moved gently to her office chair, sitting

slowly, resting her elbows on the charred surface of the table and knotting her fingers together. She looked at him across a shallow drift of extinguisher residue and sighed. 'You're a smart boy, you know. Is there any point in asking why you keep doing this?'

Nothing.

'Any point in asking you to stop?'

Nothing, and somehow even less.

'Right. Well, I'm not entirely sure what to do with you,' she lied. Slowly, she eased herself out of the chair and moved back to the window, restless. On the yard below, the kids had finally formed neat lines and were partaking in a call-and-response roll call. It looked as though the swimming team had finally been given some towels. 'St. Adjutor's took you in after everything your mother put you through, offered you safety – sanctuary – and we've continued to do so, despite your continued attempts to ignite the building.'

She looked at his hazy reflection in the glass of the window and shook her head. It was difficult not to feel some degree of pity for the boy.

'Never once a classroom,' she said quietly, 'nor a room where anybody might be harmed. Always empty rooms, cupboards, always near extinguishers, near water… you've cost us a lot of money, boy, but I have to believe that you never meant anybody any harm. Would that be true?'

The boy shrugged again, his reflection copying the

gesture half-heartedly in the soot-stained window.

'All right. Well, either way, I'd like to take action. The easter holidays are fast approaching, and usually you'd be here with the other children who've no homes to return to. But I think a programme of exercise, of some slightly more *worldly* education, might be useful to you. And, of course, I'd like you to help us with some of the replacement costs. Does that sound fair?'

The boy blinked. Finally, his mouth parted; he spoke: 'I don't have any money.'

Mother Brunheldt smiled thinly. 'Oh, don't worry,' she said, looking out past the playground and into the fields beyond, blooming at the edges with the first smatterings of Spring colour. On the horizon, a small smudge of farmhouse red bristled in the sunlight. 'I think we can figure out some sort of arrangement.'

2

The blades of the ride-on whirred loudly beneath him, the old red Mountfield rattling as it chopped through thick clumps of glass and spattered their remains across the lawn. The shadow of the barn fell across Joel's back as he ploughed the mower slowly forward, hugging the electric fence that separated this field from the next, in which a small herd of sheep calmly grazed and slept in the morning sunlight. Petrol fumes clogged the air and with the smell of grass combined into a thick, cloying haze around him.

The day had already grown unusually hot and the cracked leather seat seared his back and rump as the machine juddered his whole body, his palms sorely gripping the wheel. A brown corduroy baseball cap largely kept the sun out of eyes, but every now and then a yellowish flare made him turn his eyes down into the grass. Joel's legs and arms were stiff from collecting firewood in the woods at the edge of the extensive plot of farmland the night before; it was nice to sit for a while – and it would be a while, with the amount of ground to cover – but he knew that he would grow bored long before he was finished.

He looked around, clocking the farmhouse to his right: a decrepit heap of jutting boards and exposed brickwork, the tiny kitchen window glinting, the slanted roof poking into angular outcrops where the attic rooms sprung up from the thatch. To his left, the fence broke away and a wide dirt path lined with trees curved slowly toward the village. As he passed the shadowy path and continued along the fence, he watched more sheep amble slowly through the next field and heard, very faintly beneath the roar of the Mountfield's engine, the occasional *crack!* of the electric fence.

Briefly Joel was distracted by the sight of a dark, pointed building on the horizon – between dark scraggles of woodland, beyond the fields – that he thought might be the academy, and almost didn't see the body.

A fly alighted on his cheek like a clump of iron filings drawn to an electromagnetic. He slapped at it, turning his attention back to the grass directly ahead of the mower – and his eyes widened as he saw the carcass in the grass.

Quickly Joel stamped on the mower's brake and slowed the rattling thing before it passed right over the body. As the blades slowed, he turned off the sputtering engine and sat for a moment in the silence, staring down at the thing he had almost run over. He had already gone over two of the things in the last week or so, and he hated the sound of bones crunching up in the rotor. What was worse, though, was the way it spat out clumps of bloody fur and popped, slippery organ and the smell of decay that followed as the blades flung strings of blood into the grass.

Reluctantly Joel stepped down off the ride-on and approached the body, batting away the flies that buzzed relentlessly above it.

'Well, shit,' he said quietly, standing over the carcass with his hands on his hips.

The rabbit stared eyelessly up at him, its limbs bent and tangled in the grass, its face and stomach already pocked with holes where the flies had begun to chew through its fur. Sunlight gathered in the congealed skin of tiny beads of blood that had oozed up from the tiny wound in its neck, a deep black hole where the air-rifle pellet had passed through it.

'At least there's no maggots on this one,' Joel grunted, bending down and reluctantly digging his hand beneath the carcass's belly to scoop it up. Immediately he withdrew as a dozen wriggling shapes fell into his hand, dropping from a pit in the thing's stomach. 'Wrong,' he sputtered, retching as he backed away. 'Wrong, I was wrong.'

He doubled over, cringing at the sour taste of bile in his throat and the lingering feeling of tiny, damp bodies writhing against his flesh.

Straightening, he returned to the body and gingerly extended a discoloured arm. Plucking a loose sheath of fur around its ribs, he pinched the skin into a crude, still-warm carry handle and lifted the poor dead thing out of the grass, ignored the little clump of plump wiggling shapes that fell from its open belly. He carried it past the silent mower, trying not to look down at his hand. He had grown less squeamish about the things in his first week here, but physically picking them up still disturbed him a little.

Quickly he took the rabbit across the field toward a gate in the fence, which he opened one-handed and passed through quite awkwardly. Heading toward the barn, he stopped when he reached a large patch of ashen, barren earth in the grass. Here an assortment of pieces of old wood and cardboard had been arranged into a dull brown mountain, sawn-off branches and logs piled up beneath the larger slabs.

'Another one bites the dust,' he murmured, tossing the rabbit into an awful, stinking mound of grey-brown fur at the base of the pile. A tiny clot of ash puffed up around it as it landed limply on the ground.

The black, blank eyes – those that hadn't been chewed out by flies – of a dozen more little carcasses stared dimly up at him, each body marked by a single pellet hole.

3

Rudy took one end of the bench as Joel lifted the other and together they carried it from the porch, heading toward the barn. The old man must have been in his late sixties, if not gone seventy, but he had retained much of his strength: his neck and arms were scrawny but thick cables bulged beneath the skin; they only had to stop and lay the bench down once, halfway across the field. As they did Joel readjusted the rucksack on his shoulder, and the old man cracked his back and popped his knuckles, one by one. Behind him the sun finally succumbed to the magnetic pull of the horizon and dropped beneath the tree line. Banks of orange and pink had begun to fade to a visceral bruise-purple. Clouds hung the moon, half-visible, above the farmhouse behind them.

'Ready to go again?' Rudy said, his voice shot like he still had a dozen smouldering cigarette butts in a little hoarse throat-pocket. Joel nodded, and they heaved the bench up again and continued. The old man kicked the gate open as they reached it and they swung the bench through, turning it to face the barren square of earth and setting it heavily in the grass.

As the sky darkened they got everything set up. Joel slung the rucksack onto the bench and dug inside it, withdrawing a rattling disposable barbecue, still in its plastic wrapping, along with a pair of dinner plates and a carrier bag full of food. While Rudy moved around the mound of wood and cardboard before them, adjusting it to make space for oxygen, Joel sat and buttered two bread rolls.

He watched the old man curiously, wordlessly. He had taken to Rudy more than he'd expected. He had run the farm for years and years, probably born here, and his leathery face was tanned from being outside all day every day. He put Joel to work early every morning, an the work was hard, but the old man never failed to get out there too: if Joel was mucking out the sheep, he would see Rudy hammering away at some fencepost or sawing wood beside the barn; if Joel was raking the last of winter's crusted leaves from the path, Rudy would be up on the farmhouse roof patching up the thatch.

Rudy came back to the bench after a few moments

and ripped open the barbecue's wrapping, setting it on the floor by their feet. He produced a small yellow box of matches from his shirt pocket and lit one, bright points of orange reflected in his eyes as the tiny flame flared up. He lit the barbecue and together they watched the lighting paper smoulder brightly at the edges and shrink into a blackened scrap before disappearing altogether. Flames licked the foil edges of the barbecue and Rudy sat back, shoving his hands deep into the pockets of his overalls.

'Give that little sucker twenty minutes,' he said in his low, rough British-Tom-Waits voice. 'I'll get the big fella lit in a second and we can have ourselves a little show.'

Behind them the moon glowed brightly, shedding its purple cloud-skin bit by bit. Pale blue light gleamed on the barn doors.

Wordlessly Joel sat and stared at the miniature fire at their feet, captivated by the movements of the flames. Gently he reached up and pushed the brim of his corduroy cap out of his eyes. They were the same bright green as his mother's, and sometimes glinted with the same wickedness, but everything else – his nose, slightly bent to the left; his ears, pointed outward like rocket fins – was his dad's.

He looked up to see Rudy watching him, the old man's tufty white hair lit blue by the moonglow, little scraps of wiry orange light from the barbecue flames scattering the stubble on his chin and sallow, withdrawn cheeks.

'What?' Joel said, not with the same sourness with which he spoke to the nuns but a genuine intrigue.

Rudy shook his head. 'Nothing,' he said, looking out at the barn. 'How you finding it here, kid?'

Joel shrugged. 'It's hard work,' he said, 'but it's fine. I don't mind.'

'I'm sure you'd have complained if you did.'

'I like work like this,' Joel said. 'I don't want to grow up and sit in an office.'

'You know what you wanna be?'

He shook his head, reaching up to tug the brim of his cap down again. His eyes fell into shadow, thick sandy hair springing up at the back of his skull. 'Nah.'

'You got time. How old are you, kid?'

'Sixteen.'

'Well, you got time.'

They sat in silence for a few minutes, then Rudy nudged the little trashy barbecue with his boot and said it was probably ready. Joel unwrapped a two-pack of pork and apple burgers and dropped them gently onto the grille. The raw red meat sizzled immediately, and they watched as bubbles of fat plopped into the white coals beneath.

'You want to light the fire?' Rudy said after a minute or so, nodding toward the heap of rotten wood and scraps spread across the ashen patch of earth. They had set the bench down about six feet from it, and though the heat would reach them nicely Joel knew the smoke wouldn't. They had done this twice now, in the week that he'd been here, and both times Rudy had marked a spot for the bench that, somehow, seemed to be completely out of the wind.

Joel paused. He felt the small weight of the thing in his jeans pocket and swallowed.

'I know I ain't supposed to let you light it,' Rudy said, 'but I don't think you're about to burn my fuckin farm down, now, are you?'

Joel shook his head.

Rudy dug in his shirt pocket and handed the yellow matchbox to the boy. 'Here, then,' he said, 'if you want.'

Joel nodded, cautiously taking the matches. He stood up and stepped past the sizzling barbecue, moving carefully toward the crude firepit. His heart fluttered gently against his ribs. He hesitated, remembering the look on Mother Brunheldt's face when she'd had him dragged to the office. Well, what did that matter? There was a difference between lighting a ball of paper in the caretaker's desk and setting an actual fire.

He just wanted to watch the flames.

Aware of Rudy's eyes on his back, Joel tucked the matchbox into his jacket pocket and reached into his jeans. Eyes down, he produced a small, steel lighter and flipped open the lid. He glanced back in Rudy's direction and the old man nodded.

Turning back to the firepit, Joel crouched on his heels and drew in a breath. Gripping the lighter firmly, he snapped the spark wheel with a sharp roll of his thumb and the wick ignited. Thrusting his arm forward, he held the flame to a thick sheet of cardboard lodged firmly in the centre of the heap. After a few moments the cardboard caught, and within a minute the tiny flames had licked all the way up it.

Stepping back, Joel poked the lighter back into his pocket and watched the fire spread.

Logs caught and, within minutes, began to bubble as sap oozed like foam from cracks in the wood. Green branches caught quickly and burned bright yellow, leaves shrivelling like molten plastic. The smell of smoke became a haze around him and the wall of the barn beyond the firepit was illuminated with soft shafts of flickering amber. The dark behind him was thick and blue and oppressive but all around him the warm glow of the flames scratched a spotlight in the earth; the heat was enveloping and decadent. He couldn't help but see traces of his father's face in the flames. He thought if he stared too deeply into them he might cry a little.

Joel returned to the bench and sat, hands in pockets, his eyes locked on the fire. Beside him Rudy was awkwardly trying to flip each burger with his thumbs and not burn his skin. The old man said, not looking up: 'Feel better?'

'Fine,' Joel said quietly.

The flames danced slowly, hypnotically, over ridges of wood and fibre, glaring at their core and whispering in dark shades of orange at edges that constantly moved and writhed. The smoke-smell was broken by hints of burning meat and his eyes were drawn down to the little pile of rabbit carcasses half-buried in the smouldering detritus. Fur alight, they caught slow and burned fast, meat and organs boiling, moisture draining from their little bodies.

'Why do you shoot them?' the boy asked suddenly. 'I mean, I get it. Pest control. But why go so hard on them? You must know you'll never get them all.'

'You think I go hard on them?'

'Well, I just mean… if you're not working on something else, you're up in the attic pointing your gun at a rabbit. Always, every day. It's like it's personal.'

Rudy smiled grimly, licking hot raw fat off his fingers as he leaned back. The firelight cast a thick, bright spell over them, crackling loudly as plumes of smoke rose into the air. 'Personal,' he said quietly. 'No, I just… I'll tell you what, it's just the time of year.'

'Spring?'

'Easter.'

'You don't like Easter?'

21

'Do you?'

Joel paused. 'I'm indifferent,' he said truthfully.

'Well, be glad the nuns ain't beat it into you any harder than they did.' He sighed. 'All it is, son, is that I just don't appreciate them rabbits digging up my lawn, I don't appreciate them shitting all over. And… well, to tell you the truth, they remind me of something I don't appreciate thinking about. That's all.'

'Fair enough,' Joel said.

Rudy leaned forward and poked one of the burgers, wincing as the hot, bubbling meat seared the pad of his finger. 'Think these're about there?' he said.

'Look good to me,' Joel said, handing the old man a plate and a buttered roll.

Together they ate, watching the fire as the sky was shot through with stars. There was something about the heat on his face, Joel thought, while his back was chilled by the night wind. The meat was good: sweet and gamey, almost melting on his tongue. His body was sore from work but it was a good kind of sore.

After an hour or so the fire began to dwindle. Rudy had fallen asleep, his head tipped forward, and his snoring was interrupted by regular popping sounds that seemed to come from the same scorched pocket in his throat where he stored all his cigarette butts.

Eventually Joel grew restless. He reached up to remove his cap, running a hand through his hair before stuffing it into his pocket and standing off the bench.

He moved closer to the fire, looking into its heart, watching as the brilliant white glow in its centre spilled softly into little mounds of ash. Puffing air through his cheeks, he began to wander toward the barn, stretching his aching legs.

The soundtrack of Rudy's snoring faded a little as he paced the perimeter of the barn. Somewhere close by he heard sheep bleating to one another; he fancied given enough time he would grow so used to that sound that he hardly noticed it at all. A sick pit opened in his stomach as he remembered he'd be going back to St Adjutor's in a couple of weeks, and he quickly pushed his thoughts off that particular cliff and kept walking.

As he turned the last corner of the barn and the fire came into view again, he noticed something in the ground.

Frowning, Joel bent down to look closer. A little divot in the earth, a pawprint of some kind, scuffed and ragged at the edges. Hesitantly he pushed aside a little furrow of compressed grass to reveal the print in its entirety.

'Weird,' he murmured. Looking up, he saw another print three or four feet away, and beyond that another. He stood.

They were like rabbit prints in shape, the same as the ones that pocked the dirt path and appeared sometimes in the grass where the mud beneath was damp. But rabbit prints were about the size of a twopence piece – if that – and these…

Bending down again, he laid his hand in the grass, splaying his fingers until they filled the shallow imprint.

Resolving to ask Rudy what kind of animal could have made them when the old man woke up, Joel returned to the fire and, within a few minutes, forgot all about it.

4

The soft roar of an engine knifed through the mid-morning silence like butter as a battered, silver truck rattled toward the farmhouse, tyres churning the dirt of the path as shafts of tree-shadow fell across the hood.

Joel looked up, tipping up the brim of his cap to see better. He'd been sowing a small beetroot plot all morning and stood with the hoe in one hand as he looked toward the path, watching the truck approach. Crisp, black soil settled beneath his feet, soft enough that he thought if he stood still for too long he might somehow be sucked down into it.

The truck stopped at the end of the path and both doors swung open, a young, tall Black man and red-haired woman stepping out. Both were dressed in the same uniform, crisp burgundy polo shirts emblazoned with some kind of logo. The redhead had opted to wear a sleek blue gilet on top, while the man seemed content in just the shirt. Both wore black jeans.

Closing the cab door, the woman clapped her hands together, calling something to her partner that Joel couldn't quite hear, and moved around the vehicle to the truck-bed, disappearing from view in the shade of the trees. The man looked around, hands on his hips, and saw Joel watching. His arm shot up and he waved cheerfully, teeth flashing as he grinned.

'Morning!' the man called.

Joel hesitantly raised his own arm, waving a little less enthusiastically. His eyes shifted to the woman as she reappeared, carrying a bulging hessian sack in each hand. From here they looked to be full of potatoes, but where one was split open at the top sunlight glinted off scraps of coloured foil. Joel frowned, lowering his arm.

Setting one of the bags down, the red-haired woman glanced in Joel's direction then turned to her partner. They spoke quietly. After a moment the man shook his head, pointing at the farmhouse. The woman nodded, swinging the hessian sack over her back and throwing a cheery wave in Joel's direction. Then she turned and headed in the direction of the barn.

Joel watched expressionless as the tall man approached him. Over by the truck, the redhead had stopped, and his gaze shifted to her again as she dipped a hand into her bag, removed something, and deposited it in a little nook between two thick branches of a tree.

'What's she doing?' Joel called as the tall man came near.

The man looked back, then smiled at Joel. 'I'm guessing you don't run this place,' he said. 'Sorry, that came out all wrong, I don't mean to be snooty. I just mean… I assume the owner knew we were coming?'

He reached the beetroot plot and Joel raised a hand to stop him coming any closer. Pointing down, he said, 'Just planted. Watch where you step.'

The man nodded his understanding, putting out his hands. At the edge of the field, the red-haired woman had bent down to place something small and shiny in a little tuffet of grass by one of the fenceposts.

'Don't suppose you'd be able to let Rudy know we came by?' the man said, scratching the back of his neck as he squinted in the sunlight. 'I know the old man doesn't have much to do with the hunt, but if you could just say—'

'Hunt?' Joel said, scrunching up his nose.

'The egg hunt,' the man said. He jerked a thumb over his shoulder. 'That's what Jenny's doing, planting a few eggs.'

Joel shook his head.

'We're from Bingo Fun,' the man said, as if that would explain everything. He tapped the logo on his shirt, emblazoned with white stitching. 'Me and Jen come by this time every year to run a few Easter egg hunts for the kids, you know? The first lot should be coming by tomorrow morning, so we just came along to get set up. Hide a few surprises around the place. We'll be here again tomorrow with the parents to make sure everything goes okay, and when they've all gone home we'll plant a few more eggs for the next day.'

Joel smiled weakly. 'And Rudy's all right with that?'

'How'd you mean?'

'Well, him and Easter. You know.'

The man glanced up toward the farmhouse behind them and shrugged. 'To tell you the truth,' he said quietly, 'I don't know if the old man has much choice. It's those girls at St. Adjutor's that make all this happen. They've had Bingo Fun come and run these egg hunts on this land every Easter for the past ten years.'

'What, do they own the land or something?'

'Must have some kind of arrangement with him,' the man said. 'I don't know, to be fair. Mike, by the way.'

He stuck out a hand. Cautiously Joel took it and shook briefly. 'I'll let him know you were here.'

'Thanks, pal,' Mike said, then he beamed brightly. 'All right, well, I'd better go help Jen set up. You just come shout if there's any problems, yeah?'

Joel nodded.

There was a loud, hollow *crack!* above them and

Mike jolted, looking up toward the sound. Joel followed his gaze slowly and saw Rudy hunched in the attic window, chewing on a cigarette as he poked an air rifle out through the opening. A thin wisp of smoke rolled out of the barrel and Joel looked in the direction it was pointing. A small grey body lay thrown against one of the fenceposts, blood pulsing gently from a little hole in its head.

Rudy withdrew the air rifle and called down. 'You mind clearing that up for me, kid?'

Joel threw up his hand, thumb sticking straight up.

'Good boy!' Rudy called, then he slunk back into the attic and the window slammed behind him.

Mike swallowed. 'Jen said something about this on the way here. He, uh… he won't be up there doing that when the kids come, will he?'

'I can't promise anything,' Joel said, standing his hoe in the soft earth. Resigned, he rolled up his sleeves and stepped past Mike toward the rabbit.

5

Joel's mother had taught him two things – or two that he remembered, at least – while she'd been around: the first was that life isn't fair, and it certainly isn't for everyone. The second was how to make an incredible mushroom omelette.

He stood over the old stove in Rudy's kitchen and prodded a smashed mess of egg and grated cheese with a bent spatula, butter foaming at the edges of the bubbling yellow pool in the pan. Beside him he'd made up a mix of finely-sliced mushroom, spring onion and pepper, and it lay in a small colourful pile on the chopping board with Rudy's prize butcher knife, the blade glinting wickedly in the flickering gaslight of the kitchen.

Mother Brunheldt sat at the wooden table behind

him, her presence imposing and dark even as she slouched in the wicker chair Joel had dragged through from the other end of the farmhouse. She had brought a thick, leather-bound folder with her and laid it between herself and Rudy on the table, and as Joel cooked they discussed its contents quietly. Rudy had been in a foul mood for most of the afternoon, and Joel had gotten the sense that the old man enjoyed the nuns' twice-monthly visits even less than he would. The boy wasn't curious enough to listen in too intently on their hushed conversation, but they seemed to be going through some complex ledger of accounts. Sister Emmanuel had come too, but for most of the evening she had stared wordlessly at the back of Joel's head from her own place at the table, and now had disappeared to the lavatory.

Joel dug his spatula deep into the pan, nudging it blade-like through the yellow mess and drawing crude patterns in the sizzling egg with a single corner. He could feel Mother Brunheldt's eyes on his back, even as she spoke with Rudy, and knew that this little visit was about more than accounts. Rudy had said she usually came alone; Joel wondered if Sister Emmanuel was here to bear witness if he suddenly tipped the pan out and set fire to the old man's kitchen. Well, if they really thought so little of him…

Absent-mindedly he tipped the mushrooms into the pan and let the smell rise into the air, steam pluming before him. The smell reminded him of home – home when home had meant safety – and he remembered cooking for the first time, spilling raw egg over the hob and looking up to see nothing but kindness in his mother's eyes. Not the anger he'd expected but a glazed, happy kind of softness. He knew now that it was half a bottle of Smirnoff, but at the time he hadn't recognised the smell, had probably assumed the glass in her hand was full of water. He'd just been relieved that she hadn't smacked him.

'How we doing there, kid?' said Rudy, suddenly beside him. The old man clapped a hand softly on his shoulder and squeezed, his voice calm and gravelly. 'Don't fret, the Penguin's gone to find Sister Sinister so we've got a second.'

'The Penguin?' Joel asked dumbly.

'You never seen The Blues Brothers?'

'No.'

'Jesus, who raised you?'

Joel winced.

'Sorry, kid, I don't mean…' Rudy glanced over his shoulder at the sound of clipped heels on the rough brickwork floor and nodded politely in the direction of the kitchen doorway. Joel looked back and saw that Mother Brunheldt and Sister Emmanuel had returned; he smiled thinly in the former's direction and turned back to his frying pan as they moved to sit at the table. 'Anyway, you doing all right?'

'Yeah,' Joel said quietly. 'Nearly there.'

'Good boy,' Rudy said, squeezing his shoulder again before turning and disappearing from the boy's eyeline. Joel slid his spatula into the pan and folded cooked egg over a gently-frying heap of colour. The old man clapped his hands together as he returned to the table. 'Either of you girls fancy a drink?'

Joel remembered sitting at the table and eating, the smell of mushroom almost cloying it was so thick. His mother was vacant and elsewhere, cutting buttered bread and slipping chunks into her mouth between sips of wine. His father eyed her with the kind of wary look on his face that a boy with a big stick might wear when approaching a snoring grizzly bear.

He blinked, turning the omelette over and smashing the spatula into it, enjoying the thick hot sizzling sound that followed.

'It'll be ready in a minute,' he called over his shoulder. Behind him Mother Brunheldt was sliding her leather portfolio into the bag she'd brought; Rudy set down four plates and a fifth, in the middle of the table, with bread and salad.

'How domesticated you've become,' Sister Emmanuel said hotly.

'He's been rather good,' Rudy said, sliding back into his seat and ignoring the nun's brusque tone. 'Gets up right at dawn in the mornings with no complaint, cracks on with his chores like a right seasoned farmhand. Seems t'enjoy it, too.'

Joel stepped back from the stove, removing the pan and setting it down on a wire rack nearby. The kitchen counters were crudely-shaped wood, the cupboard doors splintered and knotted. A little fading sunlight filtered in through a narrow window above the washbasin, illuminating the cracked flagstones that rolled and jutted over a ruined dirt floor beneath. The gas lamp above the door cast warm, amber shadows over it all and gleamed off of rusted brass doorknobs and handles.

'Is that right?' Sister Emmanuel said, cocking an eyebrow as she looked in the boy's direction. 'You're enjoying yourself here?'

Joel looked up, nodding slightly. 'Sure,' he said. Mother Brunheldt remained silent, but he could feel her eyes on him, vaguely see her habit-clad shadow looming over the table. 'I like it.'

'Such a shame that our school wasn't such a good fit for you,' the younger of the nuns said.

'Now, girls, let's eat the boy's cooking without talking shop, shall we?'

Sister Emmanuel reached for her drink and took a long, deliberate sip, keeping her eyes on him. 'Perfect,' she said eventually. 'Let's.'

Joel brought the omelette over and served each of them quickly, by habit leaving himself the smallest piece. Returning the pan to the wire rack, he sat quietly and waited for the others to take some salad before reaching across for any. As he did, his eyes caught Mother Brunheldt's, and he saw that she was smiling. There in her eyes was the same wariness that he'd seen in his father's. Brunheldt had poked the bear before, and after a few prods of the stick the bear had set fire to her office.

But she wasn't here to poke him again now; there was suspicion, too, in her eyes, and a stern kind of watchfulness. She had the stick in her hand, but she would only use it if he woke up of his own accord.

Well, keep watching, he thought, narrowing his eyes in her direction as he stabbed his fork into a chunk of bread and omelette. This bear ain't moving, not for you.

'Very nice,' Rudy said, drawing Joel's attention from the woman. His mouth was full and there was a little doughy smattering of breadcrumbs in his stubbled beard. 'Good on you, kid.'

'Yes, thank you,' Sister Emmanuel said. 'Very… rustic.'

Joel chewed slowly, his whole body seething. He remembered lesson one: life isn't fair – and it certainly isn't for everyone – and decided not to throw his plate into Sister Emmanuel's face like a heavy ceramic discus. For a moment the four of them ate in silence, hunched around the crooked little table in the gaslight. Then Mother Brunheldt spoke.

'How do you feel, Joel?' she said, her voice at once calm and loaded.

Rudy glanced at him, and then returned his gaze to the table.

'Fine,' the boy said. 'I'm fine.'

'That's not quite what I mean.'

'What do you mean?'

He looked up, and Mother Brunheldt smiled down at him, lowering her cutlery. 'How do you *feel*?'

'Interrogated,' Joel said flatly.

'And in yourself…?'

'Leave the poor boy alone,' Rudy said. 'Eat your dinner and let him be, will you?'

'Joel,' Mother Brunheldt said, 'tell me, have you learned anything about yourself? Have you taken on board anything in particular from your time here?'

'You're asking me if I'm going to set fire to anything when I come back to school,' Joel said.

Brunheldt leaned forward. '*If* you come back to school,' she said, her voice almost a snake-like hiss. 'What do you think? Should we let you?'

Joel shrugged. 'That's up to you, isn't it?'

'Please,' Rudy said, 'let's just—'

'It's all right,' Joel said. He set down his fork, swallowed. 'If you don't want me to come back, then that's fine.'

'You've nowhere else to go.'

'Then it'll be on your conscience when I get axe-murdered.'

'Excuse me?'

'I'll be fine, probably,' Joel said, 'I reckon I could make it on the streets. For a little while. But if I end up homeless, out in the woods somewhere, and you could've stopped that? I don't think you could live with yourself.'

Brunheldt said nothing.

'Does that answer your question?'

'You can't expect our hospitality to continue if you reject it,' Sister Emmanuel said sharply.

Mother Brunheldt raised her hand. For a moment, it looked as though she had something to say; Joel could see the anger bristling in her eyes, burning hotly in the gaslight. He remembered the same fire in his mother's.

Then her face changed, and she turned to Rudy and said, quite cheerfully, 'While I'm here, I suppose I should extend an invitation to the both of you. As you know, Rudy, we'll be hosting the Easter Day Swimming Competition in just a few days.'

'And you're kind enough to invite me,' Rudy grunted sorely, shovelling omelette into his mouth and reaching for a splintered pepper grinder. 'Well, I should hope so, since you're doing the damn thing on my land.'

'You'll be coming along, then?' Brunheldt said.

'Nah, fuck that off.'

Brunheldt cocked an eyebrow, turning briefly to

Sister Emmanuel. 'Well,' she said calmly, 'I suppose that's fair enough.'

'Your land?' Joel said. 'Why would—'

'The pond,' Rudy nodded, wiping his mouth. 'On the edge of the north field, near the woods.'

'It's an excellent location for the event,' Brunheldt said, leaning in as though dispensing a precious secret. 'Such a sizeable body of water in such a natural, green environment… you should go and see it, if you haven't already.'

Joel paused. Evidently there was some kind of arrangement between the sisters and Rudy, but he wondered for a moment why the old man would put up with it all if he hated them as much as he seemed to.

Life isn't fair, he remembered, and it certainly isn't for everyone.

6

For nearly two weeks Joel had enjoyed the peaceful solitude of the farm, the only regular sounds those made by his tools or those of the lambs bleating in the fields neighbouring the farmhouse lawn; the sudden cacophony of excited cheers and laughter that accompanied the first Easter egg hunt was almost enough to make him wish he was still at St. Adjutor's with the others.

He was bent down at one of the fenceposts, the smell of varnish ruining the petrichor around him as he carefully painted the wood. Rudy was somewhere inside, presumably fixing up the plumbing in the downstairs bathroom – Joel had half-wondered, quite cynically, if the leaking pipe was a result of the nuns' visit, something to keep the old man busy while the first batch of kids explored the grounds – or going over the ledger that they'd left him. The boy couldn't pretend to understand the complex arrangement Rudy had with the nearby school, and nor did he care particularly, but he could see that the old man was hurt by it, and he wondered if, perhaps, things had once been a little simpler.

Joel worked quietly as the kids ran about, glancing up occasionally when a lamb in the field beyond the fencepost approached him warily, or when one of the children tumbled into a patch of stinging nettles and yelped for their parents. Two minivans had parked at the end of the path leading back into the village; a group of about a dozen adults stood by one of these, chatting over the steam rising from floral-patterned thermoses and tin mugs. The redhead and the tall Black man from Bingo Fun supervised the kids a little less lethargically than the parents, clapping their hands every now and then and shouting encouragements and directions whenever the hunt stalled a little. There were probably about twenty-five children, all between five and ten years old at Joel's best guess, and it felt like there were at least twice as many. His skin crawled with anxiety, everything too loud, too close, his ears pounding with every smack of a snapped branch or thump of wellington boots in the grass. Occasionally the electric fence where he was working would snap, a constant low hum of power running through the wires above his head.

'Mum, look what I found!' yelled one of the kids, jogging over to the ring of less-than-enthusiastic parents standing around the van. Joel looked up as discretely as he could, barely moving his head. The girl was probably five or six and had clearly been dressed by her mother – a white-haired woman in blue corduroy overalls with a green Kermit mug – for wetter weather; her wellies were the same bright yellow as her coat, the hood of which was scrunched up beneath an unruly mess of curled blonde hair, and she was almost blinding. She bounded up to her mother and held up both hands, something pale blue gripped tight in her pudgy fingers. 'Look at this! Isn't it weird?'

The mother bent down, faux-excitement on her face, the other adults around them glancing sidelong at the thing in the girl's hand. Joel saw one of them frown at another and lifted his head a little, trying to get a closer look. 'Oh, let's see, Missy, what's—'

The white-haired woman stopped suddenly and her own expression turned to one of confusion. She looked up at the slight Asian woman she'd been speaking to and her mouth opened, as if to say something else. Then it closed.

'Must be a part of someone else's hunt,' the Asian woman supplied with a shrug.

The girl's mother turned back to her, nodding. 'It's very nice, sweetie. But I don't think we're allowed to take that one. Where did you find it?'

'Just in the grass,' the child said, pointing vaguely in the direction of the barn, where a group of five or six kids were digging in the tall clumps of dry grass around the edges of the building.

'Doesn't look like chocolate,' one of the parents murmured. Another agreed quietly. Joel painted slowly, dragging the varnish up and down as he listened, his eyes locked on the small gathering. The white-haired woman ruffled her daughter's hair with a flash of teeth and playfully pinched the girl's ear.

'Why don't you go and hide it away somewhere, Missy? That one's not for us.'

'But I've heard there just *might* be a nice big chocolate one somewhere near that gate,' the Asian woman whispered slyly, bending forward to point past the girl's shoulder. 'I bet you can find that before anyone else does!'

The girl pouted, clutching the pale blue thing tight in both hands. 'I want this one,' she said. 'It's warm!'

One of the men in the circle scrunched up his nose.

'Go on, now, Missy,' her mother insisted sharply. 'Put it back.'

Joel looked down as the girl ran away from the group and back into the field, only glancing up again when he heard the slap of her wellingtons bouncing past him on the left. He watched slyly as she ran to the nearest tree, at the edge of the dirt path; standing on her yellow-rubber tiptoes, she grunted and poked the thing into a knotted, gnarled hole in the tree before running off into the grass.

'Huh,' he heard the girl's mother say quietly as she stood and turned back to the other parents. 'Weird little thing, eh?'

'That's no way to speak about your daughter,' joked one of the dads, and the others sniggered playfully.

Joel kept his eyes on the tree, picking out a sliver of pastel blue tucked into the belly of a clumpy knoll in the bark. All around him the sounds of giggling and rustling leaves faded into a damp, muted lull, the bright sunlight prickling the canopy above the path and spoiling the shadows.

Something warm and wet pressed against his wrist and dragged over the skin, its surface like gritty, raw meat. 'Agh!' he yelped, recoiling from the thing and dropping his paintbrush into the grass. Spots of varnish spattered his trousers as he fell back onto his rump, looking at the thing that had licked him. A pair of turned blue eyes stared back at him, sunk into leathery sockets in a smooth, black face.

The sheep licked its lips and moved away, ambling back into the grass, and Joel wiped the snot and saliva off his hand with a wince.

The electric fence crackled weakly.

7

Joel was around the back of the farmhouse when he realised the afternoon's chatter had died. Gently pressing the lid of the varnish tin back in, he stood, stretched his aching legs, and moved around to the side of the building to look out onto the lawn.

In the shadow of the farmhouse he stood with his hands on his hips, corduroy baseball cap sheltering his eyes from the sinking sun. Red tendrils of light spilled into the yellow ochre of the clouds, turning the sky into one shining spoiled yolk. Before him the recently-clipped lawn was scattered with angular patches of shadow, the silver wire of the fences glinting gently. The lambs had all been moved into one field – the one to his right, now – and on the left of the trees which sheltered the dirt path, a pale plain of grass stretched into the yellow chips and stalks of the field beyond. Even farther toward the horizon, the black silhouette of a ragged tree line bristled at the edges with burning dusk-light.

Joel walked deliberately across the lawn, abandoning the half-painted fencepost and the folded brown paper in which Rudy had wrapped, for the boy's lunch, a curried egg sandwich. Briefly taking off his cap to run a hand through his sweat-soaked hair, Joel looked about him as he moved. He was almost entirely sure that they were all gone – the minivans had disappeared, at least, and the Bingo Fun guys had taken their truck – but he couldn't shake the feeling that he was being watched.

He glanced behind him as he reached the tree at the edge of the path. The farm was eerily still, the only movement the softly-bending shadows and the sheep behind him. He was alone, completely. But still…

He shook off the feeling and turned to the tree, looking into the hole. It looked like the kind of deliberately-burrowed pit in which an owl or a small bird would sleep, and the edges were thick and dark and scratched. For a moment he could see nothing inside, but when he leaned forward he caught a flash of blue.

Gingerly, he dug his fingers into the hole, knuckles scraping the rough wood.

The pads of his fingers found something hard and

bumpy, cool to the touch. Poking his tongue out of his mouth and glancing up into the canopy, he furrowed his hand around the object and lifted it carefully out of the hole.

He gazed down at the thing in his hand and shuddered.

It was an egg. It sat heavily in his palm, double the size of a cricket ball and a little longer than it should be – more like a turtle's egg than a bird's, with less of a pronounced point at the top, too – and it was a soft, pale sky-blue all over. The shell was mottled, bumps and dimples covering it like the skin of a golf ball.

As he held it, it began to warm up.

He didn't notice at first – or perhaps attributed the sudden heat spreading through the thing to the warmth of his own hand – but after a minute, the egg's temperature must have increased a good ten degrees. 'What the…'

It started pulsing. Throbbing gently in his hand, irregular and faint movements inside making the whole thing shudder softly.

'Jesus,' Joel yelled, thrusting his hand forward to shove the egg back into its hole in the tree. Instinctively he wiped his hand on his shirt, his skin prickling uncomfortably as though the thing had split open and oozed gunge all over him. He felt dirty – the same way he felt when he had to carry one of Rudy's four-legged victims to the firepit. When he peered back into the hole, the egg had stilled again. He had a sick feeling that if he touched it now, the shell would have cooled again. But he didn't.

8

Rudy sat at the kitchen table, old pains in his back throbbing dully as he pored bitterly through Mother Brunheldt's ledger. The leather-bound file was thick and cancerous, a complex pack of documents and forms that he had no patience for or will to understand, but which had formed a regular symptom of the disease with which he'd been afflicted ever since they'd taken over the land.

Bastard nuns.

An untouched mug of coffee steamed gently beside his gnarled hand, his knuckles wrinkled and bulging, his fingers crooked and stiff. The ragged, tatty sleeve of his shirt was a splash of blood-red across his wrist. The nails of one hand rapped anxiously on the table as, with the other, he reached across the ledger for an assortment of red-stamped envelopes and receipts. Flitting cautiously through papers, he cursed whatever middle-management grub had decided St. Adjutor's ought to have ultimate power over the fields that neighboured the school. Then, quite separately, he cursed the agricultural apocalypse – recession, he supposed he was meant to call it – that had given him no choice but to accept their offer.

Thirdly, he sat back in his chair, looked toward the window over the sink, and said, 'Fuck.'

He sat like that for a while, gazing out at the setting sun and the needles of light that pricked the glass, his head sore with anger and running twice as hard as it was used to on about ten per cent of the fuel it needed. Eventually the old man stood, bolts of pain shooting into his knees as they cracked loudly. Stiff from sitting, he hobbled to the window and stood with one hand on the edge of the sink, his knotted fingers curled over the lip. Gritting his teeth, he watched the sky slop red with the familiar entrails of dusk and the clouds slowly stain and darken. Like a bruise, or the ichor left on the skin after handling a soaked red onion, purple shades seeped into the yellow.

Rudy had avoided the windows while the kids had been out there, only stepping out briefly around noon to check in on the boy and take him some lunch and a glass of water. Outside Joel was loitering around a tree at the edge of the lawn, his cap drawing shadows over his face. Rudy admired the boy's work ethic, thought he was a good kid, that Brunheldt couldn't have been more wrong about him. It was just a damn shame all the boy's wages were going straight to her.

Something silver flashed in Joel's hand and Rudy squinted into the sunlight-speckled window, lamenting his decayed eyesight. He'd seen the lighter before, usually tucked between the boy's thumb and index finger while he capped and uncapped it habitually. Some kind of comforting fidget toy, Rudy thought. All the youngsters liked their fidget toys nowadays, didn't they?

'What are you thinking, kid?' Rudy whispered to himself, watching as Joel ignited the lighter and snuffed it out, over and over again. Staring into the trees as if expecting something to leap from them. For a brief fragment of a second the old man was concerned that the sisters might have been right; what if he was a pyro? What if he suddenly chucked that light into the trees and Rudy was forced to watch, helpless, as they caught and took the fences and the grass with them?

But no, he knew better than that. The kid had been acting out in retaliation, and Rudy had given him nothing against which to retaliate. Not that he knew of, anyway. He had worked Joel hard, but he got the feeling he liked to keep busy. If the kid so much as hinted at the possibility of taking a day off, Rudy would give it to him, and he felt that the boy was acutely aware of that. But he didn't.

'Come on,' the old man whispered softly. 'Put it away, kid. Don't make me regret this.'

Outside, Joel flipped the lid of the lighter open. Thumbed the wheel. Let the flame brush his knuckles for just a second longer than he ought to. Looked up, the brim of his cap tipping back as he gazed into the treetops.

Then, coming to a decision, the boy capped the lighter again and tucked it back into his pocket.

Sighing, Rudy turned back to the table and glanced down. He thought of Rebecca. Christ, he was always thinking of Rebecca, but sometimes her face flashed so clearly across his mind that the usually-subconscious thoughts seemed to be screaming.

'Fuckin Easter,' he muttered, returning to his seat and flopping down in it like a ten-tonne weight had suddenly been thrust onto his shoulders.

9

Joel shoved the lighter into his pocket, stuffing his hand down with it and squeezing the cool metal thing tightly. Still looking into the canopy above him, he considered going back to the farmhouse and heading upstairs to bed. His thoughts had drifted to his mother again and he felt like crying, like curling into a ball and clutching the lighter tight in his fist, eyes shut against the light from the ceiling and against everything else.

With half an hour or so left of the light before it faded, he decided instead to make the most of it.

He turned away from the trees and ambled lazily toward the farmhouse, hands in his pockets, head bowed so that the tip of his cap was pointed down at the grass. Hooking a quick right, he changed course and headed for the barn. The night before Mother

Brunheldt had mentioned the pond, and he'd realised
that he hadn't yet seen it; it couldn't be far, he thought,
and there was no harm in taking a little walk while
there was still a little light.

The hurt would fade, as it always did, and by the
time he got inside again he would feel better. The
gnarled ball of pain in his stomach would have shrunk
down to its usual pea size, and he'd be able to breathe
again without being threatened with an onslaught of
tears.

And he wouldn't want to burn everything in sight.

He imagined it all going up as he walked past the
barn toward the distant trees, picturing tendrils of
smoke rising from the lawn and the fields as the grass
blazed a convulsing, electric yellow. To reach the pond
he had to go through one of the sheep fields and, as he
hopped up onto the stile and over the fence, he
imagined that he felt heat at his ankles, the nipping and
biting mouths of dozens of fat, healthy flames
snapping and snatching at him. The sky was a haze of
gritty smog, the treetops blackened, already burned
out, and the trunks snaked through with wet trails of
orange; behind him, the barn and the farmhouse
crackled, the fences crumbling to dust as everything
sagged beneath the weight of the blaze—

He walked quickly through the field, fresh-chewed
grass padding wetly beneath his feet as the sheep
scattered. Lambs bleated happily, recognising the

figure of the boy who'd been feeding them for the last week, and he smiled apologetically in their direction, withdrawing his hands from his pockets to raise them, empty.

He glanced back toward the farmhouse as he reached the fence the other side of the field. The building was still. Quiet. Untouched by the fire in his head. He blinked and then it was burning, the thatched roof caving in on itself, the windows shattering as waves of heat exploded outward. He blinked again, and the air on his skin was cool. The building was whole and pale and undamaged.

Fumbling awkwardly over the fence, his boots sunk into dry, crumbly soil. This next field was a rutted plain of brown and yellow, the chipped husks of recently-cut crops drifting lazily over a dusty dark surface. It stretched for acres, almost meeting the horizon before its path was interrupted by the tree line. Haybales had been placed at regular intervals, dozens of them rising like tall, yellow sentinels from the earth. In the very centre of the field, about halfway between here and the pond, a small mountain of the things had been arranged, a pyramid of dry golden shapes that fluttered at its edges with the wind, orange flashes of twine disappearing into a mess of split-end straws.

He walked for another ten minutes before reaching the pond and stopping to push his hands back into his pockets.

Sunlight bristled on the surface of the water, spangles of white sharpened by the gently-swelling ripples of grey beneath. The pond was about twice the size of the pool at St. Adjutor's, perhaps the size of a gas station forecourt or a decent car park; when he was younger, he'd probably have called it a lake. At its edges, ragged walls of yellow struck up from the soil, reeds swaying gently in the breeze. Thick clumps of earth formed miniature islands around the edges of the pond, eroded into smooth mounds and chewed into shape. It was peaceful, serene almost, with the tree line only a few yards behind it, the dark edge of the woods thrusting up suddenly at the very edge of the field. It seemed like the end of the world.

Joel looked into the water thoughtfully, watching tiny dark shapes flit beneath the surface. Above the reeds, a banner had been erected on two wooden poles: hand-painted by kids and covered in messy blue handprints, it read *St. Adjutor's Easter Day Swimming Contest!*. Crude almost-circles, probably stamped onto the paper with halved potatoes, vaguely resembled Easter eggs and had been painted with stripes and spots and bright red zigzags.

The quiet consumed him and he closed his eyes, sinking into it. Even in his dormitory at the school, he could scarcely remove himself from the yelling and the chirruping of kids and teachers and nuns that patrolled like wardens; here, standing by the pond at the end of the world, he was at peace. Nothing, not even birdsong, not even the sound of his own heartbeat. Just peace.

Not even birdsong, he thought half-consciously, and then something cracked loudly in the woods and his eyes snapped open.

Looking into the tree line, he saw it: a tall, dark shadow, sloughing off the darkness like skin and retreating into the woods. There for a second and gone, as though it had been standing watching him and scampered off when it realised its presence had been detected.

It was enormous.

'And probably not real,' Joel muttered cautiously to himself, taking a single step back from the pond. The treetops rustled, scatterings of fresh leaves and buds shaken by the wind. And even if it had been real, he thought, it could only have been a deer or hare or something. Everything looked bigger in the dark – and it was getting dark, now, the sunlight finally dragged away – and he had hardly seen anything anyway.

Deciding he ought to get inside before Rudy came out to look for him, Joel turned away from the pond and took a step toward the barn.

There was a sick, wet *crunch* as his bootheel dug into the earth.

Joel looked down, lifting his foot, and saw fragments of shell clinging to the sole of his boot, glued there by gobs of thick, grey gunk. 'Oh, come on,' he grumbled, digging his foot into the earth and grinding his heel. Glancing into the ground, he saw more shell, an egg shattered into pieces beneath him. The shell was mottled, like the blue one he'd found in the tree, but this was pink, a pale, pastel pink like kids' crayons. The yolk was clearly spoiled: it almost bubbled as it frothed into the earth, spilling slowly like hot tar. Grey in colour and shining, it looked like something had died in the egg and rotted.

With one last look back into the trees, Joel finished wiping his boot and headed quickly for the farmhouse.

PART TWO

GIFT

9

'Come on, everybody!'

The afternoon sun cascaded through the canopy and speckled the dirt path. Around the farm Joel heard the collective moaning of all the children who recognised the call as one which meant it was time to go home; others didn't hear it, or chose to ignore it, and continued to scour the tall grass for any eggs they'd missed.

Joel stood with Mike and Jen at the corner of the path, ten feet or so from the latest huddle of parents who had gravitated, as they always seemed to, to the bonnet of one of the minivans and had scarcely gone more than a dozen yards from it all afternoon. A couple had been dragged by excited children into the nearby field or toward the barn, but they never seemed to remain actively involved in the egg hunt for long. Now the parents, too, seemed to register that their time was up, and began sipping more animatedly from their thermoses, looking around lazily for their kids.

'Oh, I hate this bit,' Mike said quietly, then he stepped forward and clapped his hands. 'Come on, kids, come gather round!'

Joel had spent the last hour or so chatting with the two of them, and had learned that: a) Bingo Fun was a cheap Catholic entertainment company that liaised with Catholic schools and churches to provide small events and educational productions; b) neither Mike nor Jen were Catholic, nor had they imagined this was the kind of work they were doing at twenty-eight and twenty-five years old, respectively; and, of course, c) neither of them had the foggiest idea where the name "Bingo Fun" had come from.

'I guess you'll have to get back to work then, will you?' Jen said, the two of them watching from the shade of the trees as Mike ventured onto the lawn, cupping his mouth with both hands and yelling for the kids to gather round. Jen, Joel had found out, was short for Genevieve (and not Jennifer, as he'd imagined), and yes, she hated the name a *great* deal thank-you-very-much. She'd studied for four years to become an art historian, then discovered that work in that field was so scarce that she'd probably have to move a good three-hundred miles from home to find a job – and with her mother's lung cancer progressing, and her partner's work in the city, she couldn't just up and go – but then had come the first miscarriage, and the realisation that she wanted kids more than anything else, and after the second she'd decided that working with them was as good as she was going to get at this stage in her life.

Joel had listened to all of this, and to Mike's story, without saying much about himself, and when they asked him questions about school and his family he avoided them and briskly asked where Jen's partner was now (he had left her after finding out they couldn't have children, and now he was living in Dublin) or why Mike chose to work for Bingo Fun despite being considerably anti-religious (all he would say to this was that he felt he owed the church something, and Joel guessed that Mike had been in a similar situation to him at one point in his life).

Sunlight stippled the clipped grass as the kids finally gathered round the tall man in the polo shirt, each of them grinning as he went about them, passing out colourful little mesh bags in which to put their eggs. Pieces of curved, smooth foil flashed in their hands, outstretched. Joel watched carefully, looking as the kids slipped their spoils into the bags for eggs that were slightly bigger – coloured pastel blue or pale pink – mottled, dimpled, gently pulsing…

'Hey,' Jen said. 'You still with us? I said, why are you out here working for Old Worzel Gummidge anyway?'

Joel half-jolted from his little suspicious reverie. 'Burned some stuff,' he said absent-mindedly, keeping his eyes on the eggs. 'Punishment.'

'Oh.'

He turned to her. She was looking off into the field now, apparently a little upset the conversation had ended so abruptly. 'Sorry,' Joel said, nudging up the tip of his baseball cap so that he could see her better. 'I was somewhere else for a minute.'

She smiled at him. 'That's okay. We all zone out every now and then. Just don't do it when I'm talking to you, all right? I get enough of that with him.'

Joel looked back in Mike's direction as the tall Black man ushered the kids back toward their parents and the minivans. Excited chatter rang in Joel's ears and he watched as the parents tucked away their mugs and cooed happily over their children.

'I think he likes you,' Joel said as Mike headed back toward them, a big smile on his face.

'You think I don't know that?' Jen smirked. 'Well, if he wants anything to come of it, he'll have to bloody tell me himself, won't he?'

'What are you two gawping at?' Mike grinned, scratching his head as he stepped back over to them. 'I'll warn you, kid, she's a bad influence.'

'That's true,' Jen said. The other side of the path, parents fussed over their kids, maintaining a sunny façade of over-the-top excitedness while trying desperately to shunt the children into the minivans.

One woman stood looking back at the farmhouse, a gloved hand shielding her eyes. 'Craig!' she called. Turning to one of the other parents, she said, 'Have you seen him anywhere?'

'Who's that?' another of the mothers said, looking up from her child's seatbelt. The minivan was a hive of yelling and flashing colourful shapes; Joel watched intently, suddenly aware that something was wrong, something was missing.

'My Craig,' the first woman said, looking around again. 'He was here a few minutes ago.'

The minivan door slammed shut and the second woman came around the front of the vehicle, joining another man who stood with his hands in his jeans pockets, shaking his head. 'Did he go off to have a pee or something?'

'Something's going on,' Jen muttered quietly. Nudging Mike, she said, 'Did you do a headcount?'

'Of the *kids*,' Mike said. 'I thought the adults could handle themselves.'

Joel glanced about, peering into the field for any sign of life that wasn't three feet tall and covered in wool. There was nothing, even when he turned and looked into the second field behind them.

'Everything all right?' Jen called, stepping forward.

The woman looked around, her eyes wide with

panic. 'My husband,' she said. 'Have you seen him?'

'I'll go take a look around,' Mike offered. 'What's he wearing?'

'He's in his brown coat,' the woman said. 'Jeans, I don't know… he's got a grey beard. He knew we finished at four, for Christ's sake, he should be back.'

'I'll go take a look,' Mike echoed.

'You don't live far from here, do you?' said the second woman, snaking her arm through her own husband's. 'Maybe he walked back to use the toilet at home?'

'Maybe,' the woman said a little less anxiously, running a hand through her hair.

Joel swallowed nervously, watching as Mike walked out onto the lawn.

'I reckon that's what he did,' nodded the second woman's husband. 'Probably thought he may as well stay there, since we're all coming back anyway.'

The first woman nodded, relief flooding her face. 'Of course he did,' she said. 'Yeah, that makes sense.'

'Right. He's probably got the football on, hasn't he?'

The minivan door opened and a slim black-haired woman popped out her head. 'Everything okay? We should get going if we want to get all the kids home before dark.'

The first woman looked in Joel's direction and raised a hand to get his attention. He balked, suddenly nervous that she might think he'd done something rotten. Instinctively his hand went into his pocket, wrapped around the lighter. 'You work here, don't you?' the woman called. 'If he's wandering around here somewhere, could you let him know we've gone home? I'd give him a call, but I don't get any signal…'

'That's fine,' Joel nodded, 'I'll keep an eye out.'

'You sure we shouldn't go take a look round?' the second woman said.

The first shrugged, the relieved look on her face turning sour. 'He's gone home, the silly bastard. Hasn't he? And left me to sort all this out.'

Jen glanced at Joel, her lips pressed tight together. Her eyes darted toward the farmhouse, and Joel followed her gaze; Mike had ventured around the back of the barn and was squinting into the field, but hadn't had any success.

'We'll be here for a little longer,' Jen called to the woman, 'we've got to set up tomorrow's hunt, so if he shows up in the next hour or so we'll catch him. Otherwise, Joel here's got a keen eye.'

'Thank you so much,' the woman nodded. 'All right, let's get these kids home.'

Joel looked toward the barn.

Mike slowly shook his head.

The minivan engine fired up with a choking sound and a sick, dark hole opened in Joel's stomach.

10

The mower rumbled beneath him as he ploughed it gently through the lawn behind the farmhouse, cap tipped low over his eyes. With a couple of hours' daylight left, he had started to grow hungry and felt, in an odd kind of way, homesick.

Last year he had spent Easter at St. Adjutor's with the other kids and hated most of it, but there was a pit of loneliness in him that was at least somewhat filled by simply being around the other kids. For most of his time at the farm he had been alone, left to his own devices with a checklist of chores and a stern warning not to overdo himself, and his thoughts often wandered to a distance from which he couldn't retrieve them. He scarcely thought of his parents, when there were distractions around him, but when they were taken away…

Something flashed yellow in the grass ahead of him.

Gently he eased his foot down onto the brake and slowed the mower. As it reached a stop the engine stuttered and died and the machine went still. He sat for a moment, staring down at the thing in the lawn, not quite believing what he was seeing.

Swearing loudly, he hopped off the mower and patted the bonnet. The steel was baked hot and spattered with shavings of green. Taking off his cap and stuffing it into the back pocket of his jeans, he crouched down in the grass and reached out to pick up the thing.

The egg was the same sort of size as the others, about as big as a closed fist and dimpled, ever-so-slightly misshapen. The shell was a pleasant creamy yellow, smudged with dry muck and splashed with tiny red dots at its point.

It pulsed warmly in his hand.

Still crouching, he glanced up toward the barn and the firepit, the sun right in his eyes. Sweat pressed his shirt to his back and slicked his hair, his skin crawling with heat. He oughtn't leave it in the grass – he ought to take it over there and make sure Rudy burned it with the next lot of cardboard waste – in fact, something in him insisted that it *should* be burned, it had to be – but no, it was late in the day and his legs ached to hell and he was tired, and for Christ's sake it was an *egg*—

Joel grunted and tossed the egg back into the grass.

'Enough of this shit,' he said, straightening and heading back to the lawnmower. He climbed on smoothly and slammed the engine into life, propelling the machine forward before it had warmed up.

There was a wet *crack* as the shell went into the rotor, the blades whipping it into pieces and spraying grey gunk into the grass. Pieces of yellow spun away and flecked the green. A warm blast of satisfaction bolted through Joel's body and he slowed the mower again, continuing forward with a sense of victory, of triumph. He had showed that fucking egg, and he'd show it again, the little yellow piece of—

There was a *kunk* and the mower seemed to sag beneath him, tipping down as the blade caught in the grass. Immediately the engine died with a weak sputter and Joel yelled in frustration, slamming his hands on the wheel. 'What now?' he seethed. 'What fucking now, you dumb fucking thing?!'

He closed his eyes, bowing his head a little. The lighter sat heavily against his leg in its pocket, unable right now to offer its usual comfort. For a full minute he just sat, both hands on the wheel, slowly bringing his heartrate down. His breaths were slow and ragged. The iron rod of anger in his back was gently retreating, but he could feel that it was still white-hot and furious.

Slowly, he got down off the mower and bent onto his knees, peering beneath.

The rotor blades were thick, vicious knives in the mower's belly, planes of polished steel with their teeth covered in clumps of green and brown. One was bent horrifically, pranged by something solid in the grass; it had lurched down and buried itself in the grass, halting the mower in its tracks.

'Fuck,' Joel said. He'd saved himself a walk to the barn over the egg but now he'd have to go over for a new blade.

Briefly an insane thought flashed across his mind: what if it was the egg that had broken the blade? Surely not. It would have taken something hard, maybe even a stone. Leaning back, he glanced into the grass behind the mower and saw nothing obvious. But it might have been buried in the earth. Must have been.

'Fucking dumb stupid fucking fuck,' he whispered, slipping both arms beneath the mower and carefully poking his fingers into the space above the blades. He worked cautiously to unfasten the rotor and gripped it carefully by one of the blades, withdrawing it and standing with a sigh. Resigned, he headed for the fence and toward the barn.

As he tramped through the grass he swung the rotor beside his leg, weirdly enjoying the weight in his hand. He thought about abandoning the job half-finished and heading inside. Rudy wouldn't mind. But he couldn't leave the mower sitting out all night, and a proud and equally self-loathing part of him knew that he had to finish, and do well, or it wouldn't sit right with him.

The barn was locked.

'Oh, for fuck's sake,' he groaned, then immediately glanced about as though Mother Brunheldt might suddenly have appeared behind him. She had probably heard most of the St. Adjutor's boys swear at some point or another, but he knew she'd happily cane him for it nonetheless.

He was alone.

Rattling the bolt, he puffed air through his cheeks and trudged around the side of the barn, heading for the back door. It was either that or fetch the key from indoors, and he knew Rudy was protective of his keys. He'd just have to wait till the old man next unlocked, or hope that he'd left the back open.

Joel stopped before he reached the back door, his eyes falling to the grass before him.

It had rained recently, and where the earth in front of the barn was sheltered by the building and remained dry and cracked, here it was soft and sodden. Thick, dark mud seemed to explode upward from between shards of trampled grey grass, like the ground itself had fought angrily against the beating rain and the battlefield left behind was scarred and broken.

There were footprints, skirting past the barn. Big footprints, the same as the one he'd seen before: like a rabbit's, but bigger. The size of his hand with all the fingers outstretched, if not bigger. Longer, sleeker.

'Jesus,' he murmured, following the tracks alongside the building. He bent down and poked the broken rotor into the earth, digging the blade in deep so that it stood on its end. Hands by his sides, he looked in the direction of the footsteps and saw the thick, black scar of the forest on the horizon.

There was something else, too. The pawprints were spread evenly, betraying a long, lazy stride; but the left was twisted, as though the left side of the thing's body had been turned back – and beside the trail was another mark, a long, muddy smear in the grass.

The thing that had made the prints had dragged something heavy along with it.

11

The tracks stopped before the next field, where the grass was grazed and the earth constantly trodden. Joel hopped the fence anyway, ignoring the bleating cries of the lambs as he passed quietly through them, scouring the ground for signs. The fear in his throat threatened to rise like bile, to tap at the back of his teeth and let itself out, but he kept his jaw set, as if that deliberate physical hardening would keep back the terror; really, the only thing that kept it at bay was the fact that he believed, almost entirely, that the tracks he'd seen could be explained some other way. Any other way.

They had to be.

Moving quickly through the sheep, he couldn't help but notice that they seemed distressed, more so than usual when he entered the field. He looked furtively around and saw that the usually-undisturbed animals had huddled in groups, and that they watched him keenly. Thick slots of shining black opened in wide eyes, smooth muzzles clamped shut and silent. Perhaps they'd heard that it was nearly shearing time, he thought dumbly, or perhaps they'd heard the rumble of the mower behind the farmhouse and associated him with the chopping blades of the thing—

Or perhaps something else had come through here.

Some*one*, he thought. Someone else.

Either way, he steeled himself and pressed on, careful to avoid the dully-crackling wires of the electric fence as he eased himself over, using two of the wooden posts to lever his body across and into the recently-cropped wheatfield.

The tracks continued, chopping through the crumbly soil and toward the woods. He moved alongside the ragged prints, unease clawing at the inside of his neck. A spray of yellow splinters fluttered over the churned soil, inch-tall stalks crushed into the ground and bent and snapped where the heavy paws of the creature had stamped down. It walked on two legs, that much Joel could discern from its gait, but it wasn't human. Wasn't a bear, because there were no bears around here – and the prints were the wrong shape, he thought. He wasn't an expert. He was sixteen, for Christ's sake. But he figured bear prints would be fatter. These were long and thin.

He knew what had made them. He had seen enough rabbit prints around the farm.

But if this thing was a rabbit, it was twenty-odd times the size it should have been.

Joel reached a haystack and the tracks dipped to the left, looping around. He moved slower now, closing on the pond and the woods just beyond, closer to whatever awful thing he was following. It was a prank, he thought, it had to be – just some dummy wearing custom-made boots, like the hoaxers who'd made those Bigfoot prints; but what about the thing it was dragging with it? The thing that, every few feet, dug a furrow into the earth as though it were clawing manically at the ground. The thing that spasmed and convulsed, the shallow trench of its movements slopping left and right whenever it regained the energy to fight against its attacker…

Joel followed the tracks to the pond, where they again swept to one side. Passing a hand through the reeds as he moved toward the tree line, he drew in his breath and held it. The reeds brushed his palm softly and swiped his knuckles. He dug his free hand into his pocket and gripped the lighter, the pad of his thumb pressed gently against the wheel so that he could whip it out and ignite it quickly if anything came at him. Not that the flame would do much good if the thing was the kind of size he was imagining.

'It's nothing,' he told himself, 'just some prick in a Halloween costume. You're being dumb.'

The smart thing to do would be to head back for the farmhouse, he thought, but he had to know. To know that he wasn't insane.

Gingerly, he moved past the last clump of reeds and followed the tracks into the woods, slipping between two aspen pressed close together. The piney smell he'd first noticed at the pond was stronger, thicker, and the darkness cloying. He looked up into the canopy: thick knots of needles were silhouetted by the pale sun above, empty nests bulging between clawed branches and given bristling white halos. The light was filtered harshly by the treetops and didn't reach the ground; as he stepped forward he pulled out the lighter and flipped it open. After a couple tries he managed to ignite it, and in the faint glow he glanced down. The tracks continued in a direction he supposed must be west – toward the village and St. Adjutor's – and he pressed on, looking all around. Foliage crunched gently beneath his feet and the leaves rustled above him; there were no birds, no wildlife. The tracks were less clear, but ruts and mounds in the needles offered him some insight as to the creature's movements.

Tall, thin trunks lilted upward, some of them swaying in the breeze that coursed through them. Narrow beech creaked slowly as they bent back into the shadows. The floor was scattered with pine needles and snaps of broken branch, punctuated here and there with tiny bones.

'Hello?' he called softly, his fear betrayed by the break in his voice. It had grown suddenly cold and he shivered, looking back toward the field before continuing. The flame in his hand flickered, batted by the wind, dull and orange and greasy.

He had walked another thirty feet into the woods when he smelled metal. The pleasant scent of pine exploded into something rotten and meaty, and the tracks bent off to the left, slopping messily between a thick, bulging oak trunk and a cluster of spindly white birch saplings. Beyond them, a moss-coated log had fallen against another tree and its hollow shell had begun to rot into a stringy mess of innards that seeped into the boggy ground beneath.

A man's body lay against the overturned trunk, guts spilling out of a ruptured stomach. Its head was missing.

'Oh, fuck my mouth,' Joel whispered, and he turned and threw up into the earth. His gut twisted into a knot and his throat filled with bile and all that hot, wet sourness spilled into the dirt as he doubled over, overcome with vertigo. 'Oh, shit…'

When he had finished and taken a second to breathe he looked back, holding the lighter reluctantly before him.

In the dim light the sight of the carcass wasn't as

horrific as it might have been in the brighter hours of the day, and for that at least he was grateful. Still, he couldn't look for long or he felt his stomach might turn again, and so he took in the details as quickly and cleanly as possible:

The ragged stump of the man's neck was wet and drizzling; a thick wall of shining red had spilled down his chest and congealed. His stomach had been opened and the intestines pulled out, hard, and now they lay slopped in his lap, his left leg bent so viciously that the bone poked out of his jeans. A brown coat had fallen from his shoulders and lay bundled around one arm; the other lay limp in the dead, dark foliage, fingers curled into agonised claws.

In the pit of his stomach, three eggs sat quietly among a mess of punctured organs and bloody muscle. One was a pale, pleasant green, the other two pastel pink. From the cavity of the man's chest, blood dripped regularly onto the crown of one of the pink eggs, and for a moment Joel had the sickening image of a blood-red stalactite forming inside the man's body given enough time. Icicles of blood spearing through his ribs. Was that possible? What if it got cold overnight?

Joel started to back away, suddenly realising that something had *done* this, something had ripped the man's head off his shoulders and rent deep cuts through his chest, something had removed his insides and replaced them with those little dimpled eggs—

Something that was still out here.

There was a rustle in the treetops above him and he tipped his head back, eyes widening. He scoured the canopy for a moment and saw nothing. Whipped his head around, pivoting in a full circle and swinging the tiny flame of his lighter.

'Fuck this,' he said, and he turned back toward the farmhouse.

Halfway up a tree, the man's severed head screamed silently down at him. His grey beard was splashed with red, and gluey strings of it hung from his savaged neck. His jaw was slack, the bones broken, and his eyes were rolled up into his scalp. He'd been squeezed into the crook between two gnarled branches, and chunks of his brain spattered the bark behind him.

Joel balked, yelping in surprise as his gaze landed on the face in the tree, and then he slammed the lid on the lighter and ran.

12

Joel crashed through the door and into the kitchen, his face flushed red. Panting, he stumbled through the kitchen to the stove where Rudy was cooking, the smell of curry powder and fried beef rising in thick clumps from the pan.

The old man looked up as Joel burst in, shock-white eyebrows shooting up as he opened his mouth. 'Christ, boy, what's up with you?'

The boy shook his head, out of breath. Raising a hand, he breathed: 'Body… in the woods…'

Rudy dialled the heat down low, a ring of tiny gas flames shrinking beneath the pan. The bubbling half-hearted stew-cum-curry he'd been cooking sunk to a simmer and he wheeled Joel to the table, gently guiding the boy into a seat. 'Try that again,' he said gruffly. 'What's going on?'

Joel struggled to catch his breath as the old man sat across from him. His whole body was shaking, not with the cold that pricked his flesh but with the all-too-colourful memory of what he'd seen. The afterimage of the man's bearded face hanging in the tree above him burned itself on his eyes like the purple sting of an extinguished bulb. 'Prints,' he said breathlessly, 'footprints by the barn. Something big.'

'Big? How big?'

'I dunno. Bear big. Fucking Yeti big,' Joel sputtered.

'Ah. Big, then,' Rudy said calmly.

Joel cocked an eyebrow. 'You don't believe me?'

'Keep talking, and we'll see.'

'I followed them to the woods,' Joel said after a moment. 'There's a body. I think… there was a woman earlier, her husband went missing… I think it was him. He was in pieces.'

'Pieces?'

'Two pieces. Head, and… the rest.'

'Right.'

'I'm not lying,' Joel said, anger boiling up in him. Shaking his head, he pointed out the window. 'You fucking go out there and take a look, all right?'

'I didn't say you were,' Rudy said, leaning back in his chair. He gritted his teeth, chin poking out so that the knotted muscles in his jaw bulged in a way that almost looked painful. 'It's a lot to take in, kid, you get that?'

'Okay. Sure. I just – look, there's a body in the woods and I've never – like, I've never seen… you know?'

'All right, well how about you and I go take a look together, and then we'll figure out what to—'

Rudy was interrupted by a frantic knock on the front door. Joel bolted out of his skin, his eyes moving immediately back to the window. He hadn't been conscious of the fact that, at some point since sitting down, he had withdrawn the lighter from his pocket and clamped it in his fist, but now he felt the cold metal and was glad of its presence. 'Who is it?' he whispered.

'Well, whoever it is,' Rudy said, easing himself out of his chair, 'I'm sure they didn't leave that body out there.'

'What makes you say that?'

Rudy was already halfway across the kitchen. 'I doubt any kind of thing that leaves pawprints and separates a man's head from his body would come politely knocking, now, would it?'

Joel stood up as whoever was outside knocked again, pounding frantically. He kicked his chair back and crossed the kitchen after Rudy, convinced that if some enormous Yeti-esque thing did come barrelling through the door, it would take the old man down no problem at all. He doubted there was much he could do about it either, but the mania running through his body crushed that thought to oblivion before it could persist.

He stood behind Rudy's shoulder as the old man opened the door.

It took Joel a second to recognise the woman, but the moment he did his heart sank into his stomach. Her hair was dishevelled, her cardigan slipping off one shoulder. She was evidently stressed and her eyes were big with worry. Looking past her, Joel saw a battered Renault sitting at the end of the path. 'Hi,' she said, looking from Rudy to Joel and back again. 'I don't know if you remember me'—she addressed this to the boy—'but I was here earlier'—now she was talking to Rudy, having apparently assessed that he might be more likely to help—'I was with my husband, see, and he went off, I thought he must have gone home… but he wasn't there when I got in, and I couldn't get through to him anywhere – I can't get a hold of him and I can't find him and I don't know what to do but I just wondered if you'd seen him or—'

'Woah, there, slow down now,' Rudy said kindly, 'you're here looking for your husband, then?'

'I don't know where else to look, we were here last and he must still be around somewhere. Have either of you seen him? Please?'

Joel's heart split in two as he realised that what he was about to say would completely ruin her life. 'I'm so sorry,' he said quietly, 'he—'

'Oh, gosh!' Rudy supplied suddenly, smacking his forehead with one gnarled hand. 'I'm ever so sorry, I completely forgot! Your fella came up to the house while the kids were running round, I must admit I was carried away with something else, I probably nodded like a fool and forgot about it all two minutes after – you know how us old folk get, don't you? – no, your husband's fine, love. Absolutely fine.'

'What did he say?' the woman asked, her face pale.

'Something bout Dave calling in sick,' Rudy said, scratching the back of his neck. 'Said you were busy and he had no signal to text you, asked me to catch you and just say – he had to go int'work, see, said he wouldn't be home till late. I'm so sorry, it right slipped my mind so it did—'

'Oh, thank god,' the woman breathed, clamping a hand over her chest. 'Oh, that silly bugger. *I* was busy? Bloody hell, he never usually thinks twice about interrupting… oh, well thank you so much, I was worried out of my mind.'

'No reason tbe,' Rudy smiled. 'You oughtta blame that Dave, I reckon. Now, you better be goin on before it gets too dark, see, he might even be home by the time you get there.'

'Thank you,' the woman said again, smiling weakly at them both before turning around. Joel watched as she hurried across the lawn toward the Renault, already fumbling in a pocket for her keys.

Quietly, Rudy closed the door.

'Dave?' Joel whispered.

Rudy shrugged. 'Safe bet. Everybody knows a Dave.'

'Why did you tell her all that?'

Rudy looked at him, his eyes calm and still. 'You still got that lighter on you, kid?' he said, ignoring the boy's question.

'Always,' Joel said.

Rudy nodded, reaching across him to grab his coat off the hook beside the door. Stooping down, he picked up a small green bottle of lighter fluid from a shoebox of barbecue stuff among the shoes and boots by the mat. 'Come on, then,' he said gruffly, checking through the small, diamond-shaped window to make sure the woman had gone before he opened the door. 'Show me where you found the fella.'

13

Joel watched from the shade of the barn as kids ran about the lawn, his whole body itching with anxiety. He gripped a shovel in one hand, the blade dug into the grass at his feet, and every now and then glanced toward the scar of woody silhouette on the horizon, half-expecting some great clawed beast to crash out of the trees and come barrelling toward him.

Two girls in pale blue coats ran past him, giggling as they raced each other for a spark of glinting foil the other side of the lawn. The farm was a cacophony of noise: beneath the laughter and running footsteps there was a constant backdrop of worried bleating; the sheep seemed more irritable today, huddling in large groups and refusing to stray from each other. They sensed it too, he thought, knew that something was coming.

Coming, or here already.

He leant back against the barn wall and sighed, resting both hands on the shovel's handle. His cap was drawn low over his eyes, but the crisp daylight and the scent of spring flowers permeated the shadow across his face, invasive and arrogant. Watching the children dash about and scurry into clumps of tall grass, scrambling beneath fenceposts and around the edge of the farmhouse for little foil-wrapped treasures, he couldn't help but think maybe he'd imagined it.

But no, he could still smell the man's flesh burning, still feel the scruff of his grey beard as he reached up to pull the poor bastard's head out of the tree and toss it into the flames.

In his mind, over and over again, Rudy's voice repeated itself: 'By Christ, kid, I reckon we might've a problem on our hands.'

That was all the old man had said. Joel had asked him what they should do – the police, maybe? – but Rudy had simply told him to get some sleep and that it'd all be okay in the morning.

Things looked okay, sounded okay – smelled okay – but it was still out there.

Watching them.

He had no phone, couldn't call the police himself – and even if he could, would they believe him? He'd half-considered walking the couple of miles to St. Adjutor's and telling Mother Brunheldt, but he doubted even she would listen. In fact she'd probably be far less likely to take him seriously than anyone else, and if not, how could they help? The image of Brunheldt and the other nuns stalking into the forest with pitchforks and spears to hunt some unknown creature of bearish proportions was ridiculous, almost funny. He couldn't laugh, though.

If his dad was still around, he'd have someone to talk to about it. His dad would *believe* him.

'But you're not here,' Joel murmured quietly, 'are you, Dad?'

Somewhere the other side of the lawn, a girl yelped as she stood up from the grass and bonked her head on the low-hanging branch of a tree near the dirt path where the parents had gathered. A few of the adults turned, the rest continuing their conversation, and a pang of guilt struck Joel's stomach as he remembered the face of the woman who'd lost her husband. He wondered if she'd gone to the police yet. Maybe they'd show up here after all. God, were there traces of the dead man on Joel's hands? He'd scrubbed hard to get the blood off – he'd used the wire brush from the sink and ripped off a good couple layers of skin in the process – but there must be something. DNA traces in the ashes they'

Christ, could they *see* stuff like that?

'You're not going to have a panic attack,' he told himself sternly, tipping his head back and drawing in a long deep breath as he looked up into the clouds. They were moving too fast, shunted along the blue conveyor belt of the sky by invisible hands determined to mess with him. All he needed was for someone to slam down a divider, tell the next bank of clouds to slow up a little – and god, was that the world spinning beneath him? – and everything would be fine, he just needed everything to *slow down*—

'Mummy, look what I found!' one of the kids called suddenly, and he was smacked back to reality.

Joel looked into the lawn and his eyes locked on the source of the noise, a young boy with blond hair and mud smeared all up his arms. He was stumbling across the lawn, moving with the eagerness of a runner but all the clumsiness of a shopping trolley with one bum wheel. Hands out, calling for his mother with an excited grin on his face. Something in his hands.

Something pale blue.

Joel was moving before he could stop himself, an awkward forward lurch turning quickly into a purposeful jog. Of course there were more. They must be scattered all over the farm, the damn things, it wasn't as if he'd bothered to look since he'd seen those three in the disembowelled cavern of the dead man's torso.

'Hey!' Joel called as he jogged across the lawn, dropping the shovel in the grass. The kid turned his head, clutching the thing instinctively to his chest. 'Let me see that!'

The kid backed away as Joel reached him, holding out one hand to take the egg. Chubby fingers folded around it, obscuring it from view.

'Please,' Joel said, 'just let me see, it might be dangerous—'

'It's mine!' the kid said.

'No,' Joel insisted, 'it's not. That one's not for you.'

The kid opened his mouth. His eyes were shining and wet suddenly, his face enveloped by the shadow of his sixteen-year-old attacker. He looked for all the world like he was about to protest again, but decided against it. Slowly, gingerly, he reached up and offered Joel the egg.

Joel took it wordlessly and looked down.

The egg was wrapped in pale blue foil, crinkled in places and torn in one tiny spot so that the brown chocolate beneath showed through. It was a little larger than some of the others, and darker blue zigzags decorated the foil, but it wasn't warm or pulsing; it wasn't evil.

'What the hell do you think you're doing?' somebody snapped over his shoulder, and before Joel could look up the egg had been snatched from his hand.

'I'm sorry, I—'

The kid's father grabbed his son by the shoulder and whipped him away, shooting Joel a filthy look. 'Bloody disgraceful,' the man murmured, shoving the egg back into the little boy's hand and marching him across the lawn.

Shit, Joel thought.

He glanced into the trees where the minivans were parked and saw a couple of the other parents watching him, eyes narrowed and suspicious. All around him kids darted through the grass, just flashes of colour and sound. God, why was he acting like such a tit? He'd scared that poor kid out of his mind, he realised, and all because he was on edge. He thought about going over to apologise, but it wouldn't do any good.

Lowering his cap over his eyes, Joel headed back toward the barn and dipped down to scoop the shovel out of the grass. Moving to the nearest fencepost, he leaned on the wood – careful not to brush the electric wires – and listened to the steady *crack!* of energy, trying desperately to drown out everything else. After a few minutes, the sounds of laughter and running had dulled down to a muffled hum and his heartbeat had slowed again. He looked up, opening and shutting the cap of the lighter in his pocket. Open and shut. Open and shut again.

Klik-klik-klik-klik-klik-klik.

Fucking idiot, he thought. Now everyone over there thinks you're a psycho; they're probably whispering right now about the boy in the corduroy cap who tried to steal a little kid's chocolate Easter egg—

Something plopped softly into the grass behind him

with a *paf.*

It took him a moment to register the sound, but when he did he turned his head, nudging his cap back up to see.

His blood went cold as he saw a dark shape bound effortlessly through the wheatfield in the distance and disappear into the woods. It took great springing steps, and though he could scarcely make out its shape – it was a charcoal-grey colour, but the sun was too hot and bright in his eyes to allow him to discern anything else – he could tell it was big. Lightning fast, it vanished. He blinked.

Looked down.

A bright green egg had been placed gently in the grass right behind his feet. A gift. The thing had been so close to him that he'd probably have been able to feel its breath on his neck, hear its heartbeat even, if he'd not tried so hard to blot everything out.

Joel stared at the big, dimpled egg and watched it pulse softly.

14

He had grown so much older in the last few years than he should've. He'd been nine years old when it happened, still too young to fully understand but old enough to know that this wasn't how things were meant to be.

He sat on the end of his bed, knees up to his head, arms wrapped around his legs. As small as he could get; not half as small as he wanted to be, but it would have to do. His bedroom was small, cramped, but fine. Just fine. He'd never complained that his mother wouldn't allow him to put posters on the wall; he just kept all the ones he'd torn out of magazines in a little pile under the bed and drew them out to look every now and then. He was slight, scrawny, his sandy hair scruffy and in need of a cut. He was swallowed by a jacket that had once belonged to his dad and sometimes he would borrow his father's hat – a brown, corduroy cap with wonky stitching – and put it on his head, even though it was too big.

Downstairs, the kitchen exploded.

An enormous clatter of saucepans made Joel bolt out of his skin. Cupboard doors slammed shut – *boom!boom!boom!* – and the floor of his bedroom shuddered a little. He moaned softly into his knees, on edge and waiting for the next explosion. He couldn't lock his bedroom door but he'd shunted his chair against the handle to jam it shut. The monsters invading his home room by room wouldn't get him in here. They never did. Whenever they came – whenever they *really* came, like tonight – they seemed to forget he existed.

He heard a yell, his mother's voice – but it wasn't her, not really, it was the thing that lived in her throat and clawed its way out sometimes – saying something like *never fucking had kids I wouldn't* have *to drink* and then a dinner plate smashed on the tiles.

Joel's father never raised his voice, not to her, not to anyone, so Joel could never hear what the man was saying in return. When this happened it was like listening to somebody on the phone and not knowing what was going on on the other end of the line. He didn't even know what his mother was angry about, though he suspected it might be to do with the mud he'd tracked into the hall when he'd come home from school. He had wiped his shoes on the doormat like always but must have missed some, because he scraped a little smear of dirt into the carpet when he took them off.

The kitchen door exploded open and the shouting carried upstairs:

'—better than me, do you? Well I'll tell you what, while you're—'

(*the living room door slams open*)

'—I'm here, looking after that shit, feeding him, buying him new clothes – which he only goes and gets covered in filth, by the way – and you never even look at me—'

(*and crashes shut again*).

Joel cringed, sinking into the bed. Tipping back onto his spine, he rocked on his back like a beetle who'd never get up again, tears streaking past his ears and into the mattress. His ribs still hurt from where she'd stung the raincoat into his side; she'd been holding it in one arm when she saw the dirt on the floor and when she boiled into her fury she lashed him with it, again, again, again, towering over him—

'Stop it,' he whispered, 'stop it, stop it, stop it…'

The monsters were right beneath him now. The lounge was under attack. Aliens blasted the sofa into tiny leathery pieces, cushions erupting across the room and knocking something off the coffee table. Glass shattered as lanky green *X-Files* creatures swung their arms about, yelling in a language he didn't understand, didn't want to understand. The alien queen screamed and sobbed and shouted, her voice hoarse, and with every yell and wail an old bruise on the boy's body rung with pain. The knuckles of two of the fingers of his left hand broken where she'd slammed them in the door; the flesh of his left shin almost completely purple; the soft small of his back crisscrossed with white flashes of scar tissue—

Quiet.

Mulder and Scully had subdued the invaders. The living room was silent. And it was so much worse.

Joel waited, his eyes shut, hands over his face. Rocking like a baby, useless, useless, useless.

Gently, the living room door opened beneath him. Slowly, something crept out into the hall. Joel's breath hitched in his throat – she was done with his father and now she was coming for him, coming with the bottle in her hand and a book in the other – and he wished he could disappear, vanish and never come back.

Footsteps up the stairs. Slow, sluggish footsteps.

Silence; a deep, long breath trapped in his throat; a tightness in his chest that he couldn't loosen. And then a knock on his door, soft and weak, final.

Joel's bedroom door opened with a timid squeal and his father stepped inside, a hunched silhouette haloed by the light on the landing. 'Hey, kiddo,' he said softly, his smile pinched and false. His eyes drooping and broken. He'd been crying. 'You okay?'

Joel removed his hands from his ears and leaned up cautiously on one elbow, watching his father's face as the man moved across the small room and sat with him on the bed. His cheek was scratched, beads of red forming where the skin was broken. His hair was mussed, his eyes ringed with tiredness. As he sat he winced.

'I'm sorry you had to hear any of that,' Joel's father whispered.

'Is she asleep?' Joel said.

'Yes.'

'Are you hurt?'

The man smiled warmly, but it didn't reach his eyes. 'I'm good, Joel. I'm okay. Don't worry about me.'

'I'm sorry about the mud,' Joel said, 'I would've cleaned it, I swear, I didn't get to—'

His dad raised a hand. 'Shh,' he said. 'It's all right, kiddo. I know. It's all right.'

Drawing in a sharp breath as if in a great deal of pain, Joel's father reached into his jeans pocket and fumbled for something. He withdrew it and held it in a closed fist, then looked down at the boy.

'I want you to have something,' he said softly. 'I know things are really dark at the minute, but I need you to know that they're going to be better. You just have to have some way of... I don't know, some way of seeing. Something to keep the dark away. I thought I could do that for you, Joel, but I… I can't. Not anymore.'

Joel frowned. Gently he reached up and pried his dad's fist open to see what was inside.

A flash of silver. A slim, rectangular thing with a capped lid and a rusty wheel.

'Take it,' his father said. 'Please. I need you to have it, kiddo. I need you to have something to remember me by.'

Joel opened his mouth to speak, but his dad raised that hand again.

'Remember me,' he said quietly, and he leaned forward and kissed Joel on the forehead. Carefully he slipped the lighter into the boy's hand and closed his fingers around it. 'Always remember me, kiddo.'

He stood up and walked back to the door. Joel shook his head. 'Why, where are you going?' he said.

His dad paused at the door, turned back to look, and said, 'Joel, I'm so sorry.'

He stepped out onto the landing, closing the door behind him, and moments later Joel heard the bathroom door open and shut.

He looked down at the lighter in his hand. With a trembling thumb, the boy flipped open the lid and jerked the wheel. The lighter clicked, but didn't ignite. He tried again: nothing. 'Huh,' he said.

Then the bathroom exploded.

16

Joel and Rudy sat in the kitchen, the silence around them cloying. Suffocating in it together, they basked in the echo of that sound: the stormy crack of an incomprehensible ending, one that Joel could still hear as though it had happened yesterday.

He had grown so much older in the last few years than he should've.

'I'm sorry, kid,' Rudy said quietly, shaking his head. 'I don't know what to say.'

Joel nodded. 'That's okay.'

'Thank you for telling me. You ever tell the nuns about this?'

'They know,' he said, eyes down.

'And your mum?' Rudy said carefully. 'What happened to her?'

'I don't know.'

'She still alive?'

'Probably.'

The silence came again, and they sat either side of the small table with an unbearable weight between them. The stove fire pushed a soft, greasy warmth into the room and the lighter in the boy's pocket transferred a tiny amount of that heat to his leg, reminding him of its presence. Always reminding him.

Outside, it grew slowly dark and the sun retreated shamefully into its pit beyond the horizon.

16

Wheels crunched over hard chunks of stone in the dirt as the St. Adjutor's van rolled slowly along the path, its roof dappled by the shadows of the treetop canopy above. The vehicle was all-black (save for the faded emblems on one side and a long-forgotten contact number flaking off above the rear registration plate) and moved through the shadows like an omen of death; its engine was nearly silent but the plume of exhaust that followed the vehicle was dark and thick and unhealthy.

Thin grey light stippled the windscreen as the van reached the end of the path. It was the day before Easter Sunday and early in the morning, and unnaturally inclement considering the mild weather of recent days. As Joel watched the van approach from the front porch of the farmhouse, he couldn't help but wonder if Mother Brunheldt had brought the cold with her.

He sat on the porch and looked on as the van pulled to a halt, half-submerged in the shadows of the roadside trees. Even now the vehicle was still, the front tyres seemed to be chewing hungrily at the grass of the lawn over which the van hung, heavy and bloated, a carriage of famine and Bad Times.

Joel narrowed his eyes as Brunheldt swung open the driver's side door and stepped out, her habit billowing softly in the breeze, wispy tangles of grey poking out around her withered face. The passenger door opened a moment later and two more nuns climbed out; for a moment Joel half-expected more and more to flood out of the door, like clowns from a miniature car, but thankfully there only seemed to be the three of them altogether. One of the younger nuns shot a look in his direction, and though he couldn't make out her eyes he knew they were filled with loathing, and was immediately certain that this was Sister Emmanuel. Then they both stepped around to the back of the van and he heard the door open.

Mother Brunheldt was watching him right back.

For a moment there was something between them, an animosity that carried across the lawn, an extra scoop of cold on the wind. Then Mother Brunheldt took a step toward him and before he could protest or get up from his spot on the porch she was coming, marching over the grass, black robes flowing like a storm around her body. The way she moved was powerful and frightening, and yet she didn't so much thunder toward him as float; if he'd had the strength in his legs to stand and run, he still couldn't have. The whirlwind of her presence would have sucked him agonisingly back.

She towered over him and Joel cringed, peering up from beneath the brim of his cap, suddenly five years old and perched not on the splintery slats of the porch but the wonky wood of the naughty step. In that moment he wanted his dad, would even have settled for Rudy – and when he opened his mouth to say something he realised his throat was drier than it had ever been.

'Good morning, Joel,' Mother Brunheldt said before he had a chance to find the right words. Her voice was stony, no warmth to it at all. 'May I?'

It took him a moment to realise that she intended to sit with him. Hesitantly he nodded.

Brunheldt composed herself, gathering the folds of her habit before turning to perch her rump on the porch beside him. Immediately the air around them dropped eight degrees in temperature. Tearing his eyes off the dreadful figure of death-black beside him, Joel turned his head to look back at the van. The two younger nuns had withdrawn a bulging black cart and two duffel bags from the belly of the vehicle and as he watched, they began to head toward the pond. They wouldn't be able to get over the stile into the sheep's field, he noted, and would have to go all the way around it to get to the wheatfield beyond; good, he thought, let them walk.

'How are you getting along then, hm?' Mother Brunheldt said.

Joel shrugged.

'I hope the work's not been too difficult.'

'No, you don't,' Joel said after a moment.

She smiled thinly, turning to follow his gaze. The two of them looked into the distance, eyes locked on the thin, black figures tramping indelicately across the grass. 'No, you're right,' she said, 'I don't.'

Joel said nothing.

'You know, my father always used to say that the ability to work was at the core of every man, and that to work *hard* was to engage every part of one's being; to take pleasure in a job well done was to be truly proud. He believed, you see, that no matter the nature of a person – or, at least, their nature at the most evident layer, the nature that people understood them by – a little hard work could unlock their true worth. Blood, sweat, tears; I believe he thought that if enough of these things were shed from a person, then what had been revealed beneath would be the essence of who that person could be. And, nearly always,' she said, 'what tended to be revealed was somebody who knew the worth of their work, and believed themselves better for having partaken in it.'

Joel blinked.

'What do you think, eh?'

'None of that means anything,' Joel said sourly. 'That's just a lot of words for "we thought we could work the pyro out of you".'

Brunheldt shrugged. Sitting beside him in her habit, she was a mountain of black and white, a void of warmth and energy slowly spreading into every corner of his vision. Joel turned down his head and picked at a splinter in the wood beneath them, slowly peeling it free of the slats.

'Your dad never said any of that, did he?' he said eventually.

'No,' she admitted with a sigh, 'my father didn't say much, actually. I think he was what you might call a *zealot*. He drank, more than he spoke, and when he did speak he was asking me or my mother to fetch him another drink. But *I* said it. I believe a little hard work could do you good, Joel. In fact, I'd rather hoped it might have done already, so that we could bring you back to the school for the rest of the Easter holidays. I had hoped to come here today and offer you another chance.'

Joel swallowed. 'What are they doing?' he said, nodding in the direction of the nuns. One had decided that they might make it over the stile, and had clambered awkwardly over; the second, now, was trying without much luck to hand the heavy wheeled cart over the fence to her.

'They're just setting up the pond for the swimming contest tomorrow,' Mother Brunheldt said. For a moment they watched as a small herd of sheep moved lazily to the stile and began to bleat at their fumbling invaders. There was an awful sound as the cart fell to the ground on the wrong side of the fence, almost dragging one of the nuns down with it. 'I wondered if I'd really have time to talk to you properly while they got on with it, but it looks like we've got a minute or two.'

Joel couldn't help but smile at that. Their voices were muffled but he could hear the nuns arguing from across the lawn, the one balancing on the stile yelping as a single ewe started chewing on her habit.

Mother Brunheldt chuckled softly. 'Maybe five or ten minutes,' she said quietly.

Joel laughed.

There was a moment of levity between them, a breath of relief in the air, but then he stilled himself and it passed. 'I hear you had a bit of an outburst yesterday,' Mother Brunheldt said stiffly.

'Outburst?' Joel said, temporarily frightened that she'd somehow heard about his conversation with Rudy in the evening. Had the old man been snitching on him the whole time?

'You snatched an egg off one of the children,' Brunheldt said.

'Oh. Yeah,' Joel said. 'Sorry.'

'Why?'

Joel shrugged. 'I thought there was something wrong with it.'

'What d'you mean?'

'Look, I didn't mean to scare the kid, I'm sorry. I just… it doesn't matter.'

A pause. Then: 'Joel, is everything all right?'

Joel hesitated. He considered shaking his head, but he was still shaken by what he had seen in the woods. There was something out there, and… Christ, he was just a kid. He had to tell *someone*. 'I think there's something weird going on here,' he said carefully, looking up at her.

Brunheldt's face was blank, her eyes icy and still. 'Go on.'

He looked away again, unable to keep her gaze. 'I keep finding eggs in the grass.'

Mother Brunheldt laughed drily. 'Oh, I see.'

'No, not those ones. Actual eggs. Like, real eggs that have come out of something. But not a bird.'

'Not a bird? Then what?'

'I dunno. They're too big. And they're all different colours. There was a blue one, and a pink one – a yellow one – and they're bigger than chicken eggs, like at least twice the size—'

'You understand you're still describing Easter eggs?'

'But they're *not*,' Joel said. 'They're not chocolate, okay? They're real. And they're all over the place.'

'Do you have any you could show me?'

Joel opened his mouth. Shut it again. One was smashed and smeared across the blades of the lawnmower; another three had been burned inside the stomach of the dead man. He had looked for the blue one that he'd placed back inside the tree by the path, but it was gone. He had nothing.

'Right,' said Mother Brunheldt. 'Well, if that's the case—'

'There's more,' Joel said. Again he saw the dead man's bearded head hanging in the tree, wild eyes rolled up in their sockets. Blood drooling from the stump. 'There was…'

No. She wouldn't believe him. And if she did, wouldn't that be worse? What could he tell her, that there was a headless body just lying in the trees, and that he and Rudy had burned it?

'I think there's something in the woods,' he said quietly. 'I think it comes out to the farm when it's hungry.'

'And yet, all the sheep seem okay,' Brunheldt said sardonically.

'All right, well, it doesn't eat sheep, then,' Joel said. 'But there's something out there.'

'Something like what? A big multicoloured chicken? The Easter Bunny?'

Joel felt a sudden jolt of incredulity ricochet up his spine. God, what *was* he saying?

'Unbelievable,' Brunheldt said. 'I thought if I broached the subject of your little breakdown you might own up and apologise for acting out of turn; I didn't think you'd start blaming imaginary creatures.'

'There's something out there,' Joel insisted.

'That's enough, Joel,' Brunheldt hissed.

'You know, everyone used to believe in dragons,' Joel said, 'and some people think that that was because we'd seen dinosaur bones and put them together wrong, or something – you know, all these myths and legends are based on real things – like Bigfoot! You know how Bigfoot sightings go up whenever there's more black bears in an area?'

'Ridiculous. You're telling me the Easter Bunny's real?'

'Well, no, not like we know it, but that's just the story we made up. What if there's something out there that—'

'Joel, please. Enough. Enough of your inane babble!'

'But I—'

'*Enough!*' Brunheldt snapped, lurching up onto her feet. She loomed over him like a great black cloud blotting out all the light. 'What is it with these…

stories? Honestly, Joel! I came here to see if you'd had some sense knocked into you, but it seems you've had the little you possessed smashed right out of your skull!'

Joel seethed.

'I'll be back tomorrow for the contest,' she said, 'and if this attitude hasn't changed by then, Joel, then I'll not accept you back to school after the holidays are over.'

'Fine,' Joel said bitterly, 'I don't bloody want to go back!'

Mother Brunheldt smiled thinly, leaning forward. 'Where else would you go?' she leered.

Joel's mouth opened, but nothing came.

'Quite,' Brunheldt whispered, and she turned and stormed away, leaving Joel searching desperately for an answer.

17

Red clouds boiled at the edges of his vision, spotted with black and anger. The afternoon sun was bright and bloated, a sick ball of spoiled orange that smeared every pathetic wisp of cloud with furious, bristling fringes of gold; the wind had risen and it beat across the fields like a billowing pall spread across the ground.

Joel climbed up the porch and swung open the front door of the farmhouse, letting it slam into the post behind him. Somewhere above him, he heard movement as Rudy eased out of his chair by the window in the attic.

'You all done for the day, kid?' the old man called down the stairs.

'Not quite,' Joel yelled back.

'You take a break, you've earned it!'

Joel paused, his heart pounding in his throat, his blood pumping too fast, too loud. Hot and thick and angry and bright and burning. 'In a minute!' he called, and from the attic came a groan of acceptance and the creak of Rudy settling back into his chair.

Joel looked down into the shoebox beside the doormat, quickly scanning the mismatched collection of items inside, looking for something. He found it.

'Gotcha,' Joel whispered, and he bent down and picked up the bottle of lighter fluid.

Disappointment stung him as he shook the bottle: inside, the sludgy dregs of the fluid rattled. It wasn't enough.

He dropped the bottle back into the shoebox and turned to the hall, looking toward the back of the house. A rickety staircase clung desperately to one wall, lurching up in a mess of splintered edges and peeling rails: beneath it, the bolted door of a shallow cupboard, half-obscured by an occupied coathook.

Joel headed for the cupboard and swept Rudy's coat quietly aside, withdrawing the bolt and opening the door. Inside, dusty wooden shelves were laden with tools and equipment: at ground level, half a dozen five-kilo bags of feed lay sewn shut; on the shelf above, a collection of paint tins and wood oils were accompanied by a pot of thick brushes and wedges; halfway up the wall, a vicious assortment of power tools had been arranged into three wicker baskets, and stood beside a pair of thick, tightly-wound extension cables.

On the top shelf, a jerry can filled with gasoline stood between another filled with engine oil and a small stack of gardening gloves.

Listening for movement upstairs, Joel reached up and stood on his toes, poking about on the top shelf until he had a firm grip on the gasoline can. He eased it down, the anger in his skull flaring brightly as the weight pulled down his arm. It was nearly full.

Good.

Closing the cupboard, he moved back to the front door and patted his jacket pocket. He still had the matches Rudy had given him the other night when they'd taken the bench out to eat by the bonfire. Switching the jerry can to the other hand, he dug into his jeans and found the lighter. Squeezed it gently.

That's better.

Drawing in a deep breath, Joel opened the door and stepped outside.

The air was bitterly cold and the wind stung his face, instantly wetting his eyes so that by the time he had drawn the door shut, he had begun to grow teary. Quickly wiping his face on the sleeve of his jacket, Joel stepped off the porch and looked up. The attic window was open, and though he couldn't see the barrel of Rudy's air rifle poking out, he knew the old man was up there.

Shoving the jerry can into his jacket, he zipped it up tight and cradled the thing with one arm, moving awkwardly onto the lawn. He marched toward the barn without looking back, without looking up. Nothing was stopping him, not now.

He had to get it out.

It was burning him up, the same way it always had when his mother had taken the book to him. The same way it had when his father had gone into the bathroom and never come out again. The same way it had when, less than a year later, his mother finally gave him up to the nuns.

It was a fire.

Teeth gritted, Joel moved briskly past the barn and hopped over the stile into the sheep's field. Satisfied that Rudy couldn't see him here past the clump of trees at the corner of the pen, he dropped the jerry can into his hand and enjoyed the weight of it. His whole body was trembling, his skin crawling with an uncomfortable kind of rage. The hairs stood up on end, the dark spots in his vision circling, circling, circling. Pounding in his head.

Rage.

There was no bleating as he passed through them. They stayed away, something instinctual kicking in, telling them to keep back. Gasoline sloshed loudly in the can as he moved, ploughing forward on automatic, boots churning the grass.

Rudy would send him back to St. Adjutor's. St. Adjutor's would probably send him to the police. The police… well, it was up to them at that point.

Let them, he thought, fucking let them all.

What's the point?

Nowhere else to go. Nowhere else to go.

RAGE.

He didn't bother with the next stile, dipping instead beneath the electric fence. The wire brushed his back and crackled dully as it zapped him through the material of his jacket, but he ignored the smack of electricity and kept moving. Brittle husks crunched under his feet as he lurched to the left, not heading for the pond or the woods at the back of the field but for something right in the middle, something big and yellow, something that would burn.

He stood before the haystack and looked up, imagined it aflame.

The tower of bales loomed over him, a thick, blunt smear of shadow enveloping him completely. Flakes of yellow bristled at the structure's edges as the wind whistled through it. It was a pyramid, three bales high; he had climbed it one night and sat on the top, and the view of the farmhouse had been something incredible. He could see out to St. Adjutor's if he looked past the forest, and beyond even that a glimpse of the dull, colourless village.

He had read about spontaneous combustion in haybales: the moisture inside would react with the hay breaking down to heat up, given enough time, and the oxygen trapped in the structure would ignite it; the slow, agonising burn would destroy the whole thing.

Joel remembered the story of a man who'd been standing on top of a haystack when it had combusted. He couldn't remember if it had been spontaneous – wasn't even sure if what he'd read about all that was entirely true – but the haystack was ablaze, and he was standing right on top of it when it caved in. He'd sunk into the ruined, blazing structure beneath, swallowed by the thing. Because the heat was so much more intense inside, he had burned quickly, skin blistering, lungs filling with heat, crisping up like a rotisserie chicken over a flamethrower.

Oh, this would burn.

He stared up at the haystack for a long time before flipping up the lid of the jerry can with a *kunk* and starting to pour. He climbed quickly, digging his hands into the hay and hauling himself right to the top of the pyramid. Very briefly, he hoped that the thing about spontaneous combustion was wrong: he didn't want to fall into the haystack's burning heart without at least getting to set the fire himself.

Glancing quickly in the direction of the farmhouse, convinced that Rudy must have seen his tiny shape climbing the haystack, entirely sure that the old man was watching him right now, Joel tipped gasoline into the haystack and turned a full circle, spraying it down to the next level. Hopping down to the next bale he moved around the pyramid's midsection and swung the jerry can, slopping fuel onto the stack before jumping back down to the ground.

Thick, metallic fumes rose into his face as he gave the base of the haystack a long, thorough soak, moving in a slow circle around it and emptying most of the can into the lower bales. When the thing was nearly completely empty he stepped back, drizzling a thin trail into the earth.

Ignoring the matches in his jacket, Joel withdrew the lighter from his jeans and crouched, right at the end of the trail. A dozen feet away, the haystack glinted wetly in the sunlight.

Taking in a long, deep breath, Joel closed his eyes and remembered. Remembered his dad's face when he'd come into his room that night; his mum's screams when she found him splashed across the bathroom mirror.

Remembered every beating, every cruel yell. Every fire in him that he never got to light.

He flicked the lighter open with a definite *click*.

Every time the weight of that book hit his ribs; every time she twisted his hair or scratched his face; Christ, every time she'd ever laid a hand on him. Every. Single. Time.

He could picture it all, on the dark spaces behind his eyelids. Eyes scrunched tightly shut, he watched it all over, replaying scenes in his head that he'd run so many times, letting the anger come up, letting it boil his insides, feeling it in his hands and his fingers.

He thumbed the wheel and felt the faint brush of heat on his face as the lighter ignited.

He remembered every stifled tear, every broken whisper, all the kindness and patience and tolerance his father had ever taught him. And this made him angrier still. He let the heat prick his thumb, let its greasy touch caress his hand.

His eyes snapped open and he looked across at the haystack.

And he remembered Rudy, and all the compassion and benevolence that the old man had shown him, even in his short time here, and the fire in him died.

He hesitated. *Do it*, whispered every fibre of him, *it doesn't matter, none of it matters, just do it. Do it* now.

Jaw relaxing, Joel stood up and clicked the lighter shut.

'You're a good kid,' Rudy said softly behind him. 'I know that was hard for you.'

Joel turned, eyebrows raised.

The old man stood just a few feet back, hands in his pockets, eyes wet with the wind.

'You were going to let me do it?' Joel said incredulously.

'If it was what you needed,' Rudy nodded.

'I don't think I do.'

'Good. Well, that's a step. And it don't matter how many of them you gotta take, kid, if your legs are strong enough you'll make it there.'

'And if they're not?'

Rudy smiled. 'You took this one, didn't you?'

He stepped forward, clapping a hand softly on the boy's arm. Joel shook his head, suddenly ice-cold with the wind. He felt like a little kid all over again.

'Let's get you inside, shall we?'

Joel nodded, and together they headed slowly for the farmhouse, the looming haystack glittering like starlight behind them.

18

When Joel had finished cooking dinner he called out for Rudy to come down, dialling the stove down as low as he could and stirring gently. The old farmhand had encouraged him to learn how to cook something new – perhaps it would take his mind off things a little, and if not, at least he'd know more than one recipe – and disappeared upstairs for most of the evening, leaving him to it. Joel imagined Rudy could sense that he needed a little space, but he was surprised that he'd been left with the stove and no supervision.

The old man really trusted him.

'Rudy!' Joel yelled, a little impatiently, after a couple minutes had gone by without any sign of life upstairs. 'Dinner!'

Nothing.

Puffing air through his cheeks, Joel extinguished the flame and left the pan to simmer quietly. 'Rudy!' he called as he crossed the kitchen and moved into the hallway. Reaching out to grip the banister with one hand, he leaned forward and shouted up: 'Your food's going cold down here!'

Still no reply. Grunting, he started up the stairs. The landing was dark, and no light came from the slender gap around the edge of Rudy's bedroom door. The room had once belonged to the old man and his wife; he didn't talk much about her, but Joel thought she might have been called Maggie. There were photographs in the farmhouse's ramshackle lounge, and the ones on the mantelpiece were lovingly polished and stood either side of a dark, ornately-carved urn. From what he'd managed to wrangle from Rudy, he understood that she'd died of throat cancer a couple of years ago, leaving the old man alone.

The trapdoor that led up into the attic hung open like a gaping wooden maw in the roof, the splintered tongue of a ladder poking out of it and resting lightly on the slats of the landing floor. Listening intently, Joel heard nothing for a good ninety seconds, and then the unmistakeable *kunk* of Rudy's old air rifle firing.

Sighing, he went toward the ladder and eased himself up. As he put his weight on the first rung it seemed to sink into the spongy wooden floor and for a moment he was afraid he'd fall, but he made it to the top and hauled himself into the attic without incident. A little shaky, he cleared his throat and went to the window.

'Oh, were you calling?' Rudy said absent-mindedly, his attention on the rifle. He sat in his usual spot by the window, which was swung wide open. His rump was perched on an old sawn-off barstool and his elbow rested on the sill, the weight of the rifle propped up on his upturned palm. The stock was settled firmly in his shoulder and he'd pressed one eye to the scope lens to peer out onto the lawn; the other remained open and stared into the vacant oblivion of the window-frame. 'Sorry, I'll be down in just a moment…'

Joel jumped a little as Rudy squeezed the trigger and the rifle fired with another *kunk*, louder than before.

The old man barely shifted in his seat, though clearly there was some kick to the thing. 'Got you, you little fucker,' he whispered. Turning his head to glance up in Joel's direction, he said, 'D'you want a go?'

'Oh, no, I'm good,' Joel said assertively. He looked out of the window, stepping a little closer. Moonlight leeched the dark hearts of the clouds, a gently-weeping yellow that bristled with an eerie delightedness as it cast its pallid glow across the fields. The wind had died. 'Rabbits?'

'Little bastards have started coming out at night,' Rudy said, 'they know I'm about in the day, you see.

But I've got a surprise for them…'

Kunk.

'Got you,' he grinned, snapping back the lever and thumbing another pellet into the rifle.

For a moment a queer thought overtook Joel and he felt a sudden surge of vertigo: what if this was what was upsetting the creature? Its pawprints had looked so… *rabbit* in nature – what if it was one of them? Some giant mutant rabbit, come to take its revenge on the man who kept shooting its innocent regular-sized cousins?

Kunk.

Joel had just opened his mouth to say something when something smacked the front door of the farmhouse, the wet *crunch* loud enough to echo through the whole building. Rudy paused, his fingers curled around the lever, and glanced up at Joel 'Heard that, did you boy?'

Joel nodded. 'What was it?'

'I don't know…'

Joel stepped up beside him and looked down through the window. He couldn't see the front door, but the porch overhung the lawn a little, a crooked square of half-rotten slats bleached white by the moonlight. For a moment there was nothing, and then—

'Shit,' Joel hissed as a great grey shape lurched out of the porch and slunk onto the lawn. It was too dark to make it out properly but it was big – far taller than a man, maybe eight or nine feet in height, and gangly – and it was fast. Before he could clock its features the creature had sunk onto all fours and lunged into a bounding, springy run across the lawn into the dark. Long ears pressed back against its head; its legs and arms were long and bony, the joints bulbous and unnatural. Long claws danced on the ends of thick, sinewy fingers.

'What the fuck?' Rudy said, pushing a pellet into the rifle and swinging the barrel. Snapping the lever forward, he barely took a moment to breathe before squeezing the trigger and firing in the direction of the creature. The *kunk* was followed by an electric whistle; he had missed the beast, but somehow managed to hit one of the wires of the distant fence and the pellet had bounced right off. Before Joel could say anything Rudy had reloaded and fired again—

Kunk.

Joel couldn't see where the pellet went but, whether it had hit or not, the creature seemed unfazed. It didn't slow down a pace as it leapt over the electric fence in a single bound, scattering sheep. They bleated loudly as it passed but it didn't attack – just screamed across the field in a dark, smudged blur of movement.

Then it was gone.

'What the hell was that?' Joel breathed, terrified.

Rudy said nothing.

19

Joel thundered through the house and slammed into the front door, fumbling awkwardly with the handle as he tried to catch his breath. The door swung open and he staggered onto the porch, looking left and right to try and pick out the shape of the monstrous thing in the dark. It was long gone; the only shapes out there were the faint moonlit smudges of the disturbed sheep.

His eyes fell to the mess on the porch.

A slowly seeping pool of grey gunk was shot through with streaks of red and milky white, and the thick, goopy fluid bubbled softly as it slipped into the cracks between the porch slats. It was littered with broken eggshell, jagged pieces in all the colours of the rainbow; when Joel turned his head and looked up at the door, he saw that a foamy wall of gunk dripped slowly down it, more pieces of shell embedded in the wood.

The awful *crunch* they'd heard upstairs had been the sound of that creature throwing its creepy, gloppy eggs at the front door.

'Why?!' Joel breathed, incredulous and frightened. Again he looked out into the fields, and for a moment he could've convinced himself that the distant tree line had opened its maw to suck in a dash of shadow – was that the creature scurrying back to its hideaway?

The cold air bit his skin as he stood there, remembering tales of blood-red crosses smeared on front doors, second-born sons swiped away in the night… had the creature marked them for tragedy?

Was it coming back?

Was this a *warning*?

Joel realised he'd been gritting his teeth and relaxed his jaw, taking in a deep breath before letting it out again. If only the nuns had listened to him – they probably had entire shelves of books on dealing with creeps like this. What the hell was it, some sort of demon?

A mutant bear-rabbit?

'You're just going insane,' he said quietly. 'That's all. That's all it is, you're going mad.'

But what if it's real?

He had just turned to go back inside when he saw a flash of red in the grass. He froze, then slowly turned his head to look:

Three or four feet from the lowest porch step, a bright red egg lay in a soft tuft of grass clippings. It shone in the moonlight, its bumpy shell polished smooth by a thin coat of dewy moisture. Four or five feet deeper into the lawn, another one – olive green – lay on its side; a little further still, a third (this one an odd purplish colour) had been half-buried in the soil.

The fucking thing had dropped a trail of them behind it. Joel looked toward the fence, his eyes skirting between round blots of colour, and he saw that the creature had dropped a dozen eggs across the lawn as it fled.

Suddenly boiling with anger, he lurched forward and stumbled off the porch. 'What the fuck is going on?' he yelled, lifting his bare foot to stamp down on the first, bright red egg. 'Fuck you!'

He brought his foot crashing down and the egg shattered under his sole, gunk spurting outward and splashing the ankle of his trouser leg.

'Fuck you and all!' he roared, staggering through the wet grass and punting the second egg with his toe. A flash of dark green shot toward the fence and whizzed into the wire, sliced in half; the two halves split in different directions and the sick, grey yolk spilled into the grass almost in slow motion.

Terror and anger burned through him and he ran to the next, screaming something unintelligible before bringing his heel down onto the little blot of bruise-blue—

The very moment before his foot connected with eggshell, the thing split open. It shuddered, very briefly, cracked right down the middle, and wobbled in the grass. Yelping, Joel withdrew his foot, stumbling awkwardly back until his weight landed uncomfortably on it. With wide eyes he watched as another crack appeared in the shell, spearing through it like lightning.

Elsewhere, a tiny spike of black that looked like a slimy, wet needle burst through the shell in a little spurt of liquid. Joel's breath hitched as he watched a chitinous, spidery leg unfold, the black point becoming a many-jointed limb with organic, red highlights.

'Nope,' he breathed, backing away. He suddenly realised that his foot was covered in cool, already-congealing fluid, that there was a warm spot right in the middle of his sole where a sharp fragment of shell had buried itself in the skin.

There was a dreadful, spidery clicking noise as the purplish egg wobbled again and a second clawed finger poked out through the shell, reaching—

Without thinking, Joel rushed at the thing and stomped down on it, hard.

There was a sensation like burning as something sharp slid into his flesh, but when he withdrew his foot the thing was dead. The egg lay still and shattered, and a mess of tiny, bony legs and black, shell-like skin lay broken in the mess.

'Fucking hell,' Joel said, and he turned and ran like hell back toward the farmhouse.

20

He waited until Rudy was asleep.

The farmhouse seemed determined to let its owner know that Joel was up to no good; as he slunk up the stairs to the landing they groaned far more loudly than usual, almost screaming beneath his feet, and the old brass pipes running through the guts of the ancient building chuffed and cracked around him like tolling warning bells. Right outside Rudy's bedroom door, a sagging floorboard squealed like something caught in a trap and Joel froze, waiting until he was positive he could hear the old man snoring before he continued toward the ladder.

He climbed uneasily into the attic, wary that the ladder was rattling against its supports with every rung he ascended. Heaving himself through the trapdoor, he paused for a moment on his back and caught his breath. When he stood, the attic floor yowled in agony.

Beneath him, the slow wheezing from Rudy's bedroom continued.

'All right,' Joel said, clapping his hands together, 'where are you?'

He found the air rifle easily. There was a padlocked rack at one end of the attic, and he had worried that he might have to try and guess the combination Rudy had set – or worse, break the lock open – but the old man hadn't even bothered to lock the rifle away. It leant against the wall beside the window, thin barrel glinting in the moonlight that filtered in and splashed the worn stool and the rafters. It was cold up here at night and Joel shivered as he headed for the rifle, pausing to bend down and rummage beneath the stool for a tin of pellets. He found them and unscrewed the cap, shoving a handful into his jacket pocket with the box of matches Rudy had given him. Replacing the tin, he went to the window and wrapped a hand around the air rifle.

It wasn't exactly a shotgun, but it would do. Surely, it would do.

Joel snuck the rifle downstairs, descending the ladder one-handed, and crept into the hall with a growing sense of anxiety. He stopped by the front door and dug into his jeans for the lighter, bringing it out and clicking it open-and-shut a few times as he tried to slow his pounding heart. He remembered his father's face: kind and warm and there, always there for him—

Until he wasn't.

'Stop it,' he whispered, tucking the lighter back into his pocket and shifting the rifle to his good arm. Drawing in a deep breath, he shoved the door open and stepped out onto the porch.

It swung closed behind him as he moved down the porch steps, confronted by the blasting cold of the night air. He gripped the rifle in both hands and snapped back the lever, opening a compartment halfway along into which he poked a single pellet. Punching the lever forward again, he lifted the rifle and pointed it vaguely in front of him.

'Show yourself,' he whispered, marching across the lawn.

He turned in a full circle, swinging the rifle toward the trees before rounding on the barn and the farmhouse, finally coming back to the distant trees again. There was nothing out here; the creature had gone. But…

He could smell it. He had thought, when they were in the woods, that the smell of decaying flesh had just been the sickly smell of the body they'd found, but it was too strong, too… earthy. It was the smell of something else.

And it was close. The creature wasn't gone; it was hiding.

'Show yourself!' he yelled, swinging the barrel the other way. He moved forward, ploughing through the freshly-clipped grass in his bare feet, barely noticing the cold or the damp on his flesh, the bloody mess of one sole almost forgotten. 'Come on, you freak! *Show yourself!*'

The memory of a hand on his shoulder almost froze him in his tracks. His father's voice, right in his ear as though the man was there with him: 'Let it go, kiddo.'

Joel whirled round, his teeth gritted. '*SHOW YOURSELF!*'

'Let it go,' said the memory of his father. Joel looked into the night as the cold air buffeted him from all sides; above him, the crescent sliver of the moon grinned cruelly down on the farmhouse. 'It'll pass.'

She'll drink herself to sleep.

'What's the use in all this?' said the voice in his ear. Joel spun round again, raising the rifle, remembering the height of the creature; he'd need to get it in the face if the measly weapon was going to do any good. He had to aim high. 'What's the use fighting? Confronting it?'

What's the use begging her to stop?

'Just get inside…' his father whispered. Panic and anger collided in Joel's chest and he screamed into the dark.

Shut yourself in your room…

'…and it'll pass.'

...and she'll forget why she ever hit you.

Joel swallowed.

Teeth gritted, he hesitated. His father was right. He'd always been right. Joel was safer locked away, hiding. Confronting it – her – *it* – wasn't the way. No, this was stupid.

Slowly, Joel lowered the rifle.

And a tall, long-eared shadow enveloped him as the creature loomed up behind him and swung its arms forward.

'Fuck!' Joel yelled, ducking forward as a great clawed knot of a fist ploughed through the air above his head. Wheeling around, he staggered back from the thing and his eyes widened in terror.

It was enormous.

The creature towered above him, easily nine or ten feet tall, with another foot on top for the gigantic, leathery ears that sprung from the crown of its head. It was built like a minotaur, with thick trunks for legs and a gargantuan chest, threaded through with sinuous pipes and throbbing tendons. Fur rippled across its back and shoulders, and its wrists and legs were adorned with clumps of black spines. A muscular neck punched seamlessly into the mangy skull of a rabbit, its nose wet and shining, its teeth sharp and curved. Its eyes bulged madly and foam and spittle hung in wet strings from its grinning maw; blood-red veins arced like branches of lightning through the thin leather of its ears and became thick, black streaks through the worn fur of its brow.

Its hands were giant lumps of bone and knuckle, serrated black claws jutting from broken fingers. Beneath the fur its flesh was thin and papery in parts, oddly insect-like in others, segmented at the midsection like the chitinous abdomen of a beetle or a spider and glimmering like metal.

Black lips peeled back and the rabbit-thing snarled.

Joel suddenly remembered the rifle in his hands and swung it up, yelling out as he fired. The trigger was stiffer than he'd expected and the butt wasn't lodged firmly in his shoulder; as it kicked back it punched him in the chest and he stumbled, tipping the barrel up.

The pellet smacked the rabbit-creature square in the face, sheer luck propelling it right into the thing's nose. Joel cringed at the pain in his shoulder, steadying himself, looking up to survey the damage—

The creature hardly seemed to notice.

Blinking once, it surged forward. Its bones clicked loudly, almost mechanically, beneath the bunches of striated muscle packed into its chest and arms, and it sprung into Joel's chest, knocking him to the ground. The rifle clattered from his hands and he screamed as it ripped back its fists, throwing one into his chest with all the weight of its body and then the other. For a moment its face was inches from his and globs of hot, wet drool flew into his eyes. the creature roared savagely, rabid and insane, breath rancid and meaty. Joel fumbled for his lighter, the only weapon in reach, as the rabbit-thing lifted both enormous, clawed hands above its head—

'You get away from him!' Rudy yelled, somewhere behind them. Footsteps thudded in the grass as he steamed toward them, his voice loudening as he shouted: 'You leave him alone, you prick! Go on, get away!'

The creature reared up and Joel rolled out from beneath it. It looked from him to the old man and retreated, slinking back into the dark before turning and bounding away.

'What the fuck are you doing out here?' Rudy yelled, suddenly above him. He dug his hands under the boy's body and scooped him onto his feet, dragging him back toward the farmhouse. 'Stupid boy! Stupid, stupid boy!'

'You saved me,' Joel murmured, out of breath and unable to feel his arms. His chest was bruised, on fire. He thought he might have fractured a rib. 'What is it?'

'I don't know,' Rudy hissed, 'but it's gone for now. That's all that matters.'

PART THREE

HURT

21

The morning sun was incredible.

Bright splashes of spring colour littered the lawn, the shadow of the farmhouse keening back ever-so-slowly as the daylight grew to an intense cream-yellow; rabbits scampered happily among patches of wild grass. The ripe smell of manure drifted easily on a pleasant, warm breeze, a calm and peaceful blanket of misty haze rising gently from the earth. Aside from the distant notes of a crying bird, there was quiet. Utter quiet.

The farmhouse door exploded open and a young girl staggered out onto the porch. She whirled round as she hitched up her skirts and tumbled down the steps, tears streaming down her reddened face. 'I'm going with him!' she screamed. 'You can't *keep* me here anymore!'

Then she was running, sobbing loudly as her patent leather shoes smashed into the grass. Her heart pounded in her chest, the hem of her dress already spattered with muck and sprayed with dew. The roar of a motorcycle engine boomed suddenly from the direction of the village and began to grow, the buzzing rattle of a vicious wasp carrying down the dirt path between the trees. He was coming for her.

Another shape burst out through the door, a large man in flannel and hastily-fixed suspenders. Gripping the doorframe, he lurched out onto the porch and yelled after her. 'Lizzie, you come back here! We can talk about this!'

The girl wheeled round, grinning manically through the unrelenting tears. Her eyes were wild with anger – anger and excitement – and she yelled back, 'We've *talked* about this! I'm *done* talking, Daddy – I'm going, right now, and I'm not coming back!'

'Think about your mother, for Christ's sake!' the man in the doorway yelled, his face a ruined mask of despair. His hair was slicked back and his brow already coated in a thin sheen of sweat, his trousers and shirt dirty from work. 'Come back here, Lizzie, please! Don't make me beg!'

She stopped, out of breath. Behind her the motorcycle pulled up at the edge of the lawn, chuffing great clouds of soot like a steam engine. 'You beg all you like, I'm done! I'm not spending my whole life on a farm, Dad, I'm going to see the world! You'll see!'

'You're thirteen, Lizzie! You don't have to stay forever, you're just not ready to—'

'Fuck off!' Lizzie screamed, the tears slowing, sorrow burning away as she seethed. The engine rattled loudly behind her; the rabbits had all scattered and she was alone, stood in the grass between one life and the next, between the man who wanted to keep her here and the man who wanted to take her away. 'Fuck off, Dad!'

'Come on, Liz!' called the boy on the motorcycle. Evan Hing was seventeen years old and a good two inches taller than Lizzie's father; he was broad-shouldered and square-jawed, dressed in his own father's leather jacket. He had kissed her, behind the Regal Cinema, and told her they could see America together.

She believed him.

'Coming!' Lizzie yelled, taking one last look at her father, at the farmhouse. Her eyes flitted up to the attic window and she saw her mother's silhouette pasted behind the glass. The old woman was probably crying. As she watched, a pale, long-fingered hand pressed against the pane. Lizzie's breath hitched in her throat—

No.

This was it.

'Wait!' her father yelled as she turned and ran for the bike, beaming madly across at the boy sitting abreast the Harley as he offered his hand. 'Please, Lizzie, come back and we can *talk about this*!'

She ignored him, lurching the last few steps to the bike and grabbing Evan's hand. Blood pumped loudly in her ears, her ribcage about ready to shatter in her chest.

'You ready?' he drawled.

'Take me away,' Lizzie breathed, and she swung her leg up onto the bike.

'Stop!' came another voice from the direction of the farmhouse. 'Wait, Lizzie, don't!'

Lizzie turned her head to look as the bike's engine growled savagely. Her eyes widened as she saw the little shape streaking toward them through the grass. Her brother, still in his starry-night pyjamas, padding barefoot across the lawn, his eyes desperate and afraid. 'One second,' she said, squeezing Evan's waist.

'What?' Evan cried, fumes painting the air around them. 'Liz, come on, let's go!'

She hopped off the bike and stumbled toward her brother, bending down in the grass as the boy wobbled up to her and swung his arms around her waist. 'Lizzie, please,' he sobbed, clutching at her dress. 'Don't leave me, please don't leave me, please—'

'Hey,' she whispered, running her hands through his hair. 'Hey, shh, shhh, it's okay… hey, now, you're gonna be all right, okay? You're gonna be just fine without me. You don't need me, you know.'

'I do,' the boy said between sobs, 'please, Lizzie, don't leave me, don't go…'

'Hush now,' Lizzie said, planting a kiss on his forehead. 'Mummy and Daddy are gonna look after you, okay? You don't need me.'

'Please—'

'Stop it,' she said, suddenly stern. She pulled back, planting two firm hands on his shoulders. 'I have to do this, all right? I have to see the world. One day, you will too. This place isn't all there is to life, you know, you'll see that. And when you do… come find me, Rudy.'

The boy shook his head. 'Don't…'

It was too late. Already she had stood up, and with one last fiery look in her father's direction she wheeled back toward the motorcycle and climbed on board.

Rudy watched his sister leave through blooms of teary haze, his chest hitching as the sobs wracked his whole body. The motorcycle spun away in an explosion of dust and petrol fumes and then she was gone, and the sun continued to climb, slowly, calmly, like nothing had ever happened.

The dust settled. Eventually his father came to take him back to the house, and Rudy noticed that the rabbits had returned to their grazing as though they, too, had forgotten all about it.

The date was burned into his mind, like every date in his so-far-short life where something truly terrible had happened. April 6th, 1958.

Easter Sunday.

22

Morning came before Joel had had a real chance to settle to sleep. After the past two weeks he had grown accustomed to waking at dawn to begin the day's work; on autopilot, he swung his legs out of the bed and stretched, hardly registering that he'd only dropped off perhaps an hour or so before. Looking out through the window, he saw that the sky was still dark; a faint band of yellow stretched across the horizon, but the sun wasn't up, not yet. His head pounded. Surely Rudy wouldn't mind if he took the morning off, he thought, glancing down at the pillow. Or even, he thought, flopping back down onto the bed, just a few minutes…

His eyes snapped open.

Groggy, he rolled his neck and looked toward the

window: bright, streaming morning-light.

'Ugh,' he moaned, rolling awkwardly out of bed and crashing to the floor. His bruised ribs ached painfully, his chest throbbing as though shattered completely. He scrambled to his feet, his legs and arms leaden and thumping, and his knee cracked loudly.

The night had been long and relentless, images of that awful creature running over and over in his mind – and the knowledge that it was *real*, that he hadn't imagined it, that was the worst thing – so that he couldn't hope to sleep fully for fear that he would only continue to dream of it. And what the hell was it? Some kind of demon? A weird mutated experiment from some secret lab?

Just some *X Files* horseshit, he thought, yawning as he moved to the window of the little bedroom Rudy had given him. Leaning on the sill, he looked out and blinked sleep-dust out of his eyes. It felt just like every other morning, somehow, the sunlight still and unchanged, the crisp morning air slipping in through the ragged seals around the windowpanes just like any normal day. But it wasn't like every other morning, not anymore – there was something *out* there.

There *was* something out there. Joel squinted, his heart skipping a beat as he saw a vague grey shape at the edge of the lawn. It glinted, and he breathed a sigh of relief as the blurry image cleared and he realised just what he was looking at. The St. Adjutor's Academy minivan was parked at the end of the dirt path, half-hidden by the trees; behind it, another couple of vehicles were drawn up along the side of the path, tyres obscured and chewed up by the mossy hillocks of the verge.

He frowned. Then, understanding, his mouth opened and his heart stopped for the second time in as many minutes.

Shit.

The swimming contest. That was today. Listening now, he could hear the sounds of chatter and splashing drifting toward him on the wind. His eyes lifted to the distant tree line and spangles of watery light glimmered off the back of a slender, grey smudge scratched across the earthen haze of the wheatfield. The pond. The contest.

Easter Sunday.

'*Shit,*' he breathed, wheeling round to hurry across the room. They couldn't be here. Not while *it* was here. The kids were in danger.

Joel dressed quickly and thundered downstairs, pulling on his jacket as he yelled for Rudy. He grabbed his corduroy cap out of the pocket and shoved it on his head. Quickly he patted his jeans pocket to make sure the lighter was there; comforted by its presence, he rounded the bottom of the staircase and yelled again.

'Rudy! I need the gun!'

Rudy looked up from a mound of papers spread

across the kitchen table. 'What?'

'The gun,' Joel said breathlessly. 'That thing – and the kids – I need the gun, I need to—'

'You want the air rifle?' Rudy said, standing up from the table. He shook his head. 'No.'

'No?' Joel said, incredulous. 'I have to go out there, I have to—'

'*No.*'

'Why the hell not?'

'The kids'll be fine,' Rudy said, coming round the table and adjusting his suspenders. 'They're making a lot of noise, and there's too many of them – it won't bother.'

'How do you know that?' Joel said. 'How can you know what it'll do?'

'That's enough,' Rudy said.

'Where is it? Where's the air rifle?'

'You can't have it,' Rudy insisted, anger flashing across his face. 'That's *enough*, kid.'

'What is it with you?' Joel snapped. Realisation flooded him suddenly. 'Easter. You really hate it, don't you? Is that what's going on right now?'

Rudy's mouth stayed firmly shut.

'I need to make sure the kids are all right,' Joel said calmly. Turning back to the hall, he moved to the cupboard under the stairs and slid open the bolt. 'If you won't let me have the gun, I'm gonna have to find something…'

He swung open the door and smiled thinly.

'…sharp,' he said, reaching for the pitchfork and wrestling it free of the bundle of mud-smeared tools leaning against the cupboard wall.

'Stop,' Rudy said, 'think about what you're doing.'

'I'm thinking,' Joel scowled, gripping the shaft of the pitchfork firmly in both hands as he headed for the door. 'I've thought. And I'm gone.'

He nudged open the door and stepped outside, wincing as the sunlight smashed into his face. Distant laughter echoed over the lawn.

'And I'm gone,' he repeated quietly, and he stormed across the porch.

23

Joel ran.

The pitchfork was heavy, the long speared tines made of a grit-encrusted black iron and screwed firmly to the top of a long, splintered handle; rough on his hands, but worn smooth in places by hard use. It swung in his grip as he jogged across the lawn, heartbeat thumping in his ears. It was out there – in the woods, watching – and it wouldn't be put off by noise. In fact they were probably attracting it with all their splashing and shouting, damn it—

'Joel, stop!' Rudy yelled from the farmhouse doorway behind him. Joel ignored the old man and kept running, dipping toward the barn. Jangles of laughter and cheering came to him from the pond; there was a great splash followed by polite, tame applause. And the sound of Mother Brunheldt's voice, thick and muffled and crackling – Christ, was that the distortive squawk of a *megaphone*? 'Joel, get back here now!'

A stitch ripped through Joel's side suddenly and he cringed, slowing to a stagger beside the barn. He clapped a hand over his bruised ribs and looked back, turning his head to make sure Rudy wasn't coming after him. The doorway was empty; the old man had disappeared. Crisp sparks of sunlight rode the chipped blades of grass all around him, dazzling green folds of a blanket that rippled in the breeze.

In the quiet stillness of that moment, he heard it.

A snuffling sound, like a pig hunting greedily for truffles. Then a long, quiet growl, low and rumbling like the rattle of a faraway engine. But it was close; he could hear the soft, padding footsteps of the creature, and that awful, insect-like clicking of its bones…

The sounds were coming from inside the barn.

'Oh my god,' Joel whispered, turning his head toward the barn door. His eyes flickered to the bolt. Padlocked. Tightening his grip on the pitchfork, he steeled himself.

Inside, the snuffling had stopped.

Joel took a step toward the door, every fibre of his body crackling electric with fear. It was in there. He'd thought for sure it had made some kind of den or nest in the woods, but… god, had it been *living* in the barn?

The creature growled again, right behind the door. The wood rattled.

Clamping his teeth together, Joel raised the pitchfork high and prepared to barge the door—

And a bolt of white-hot pain exploded into his skull as something hard and sharp smacked the back of his head. Black stars danced in front of him and he crashed forward, hitting his knees in the grass.

24

The world swam around Joel's head as he looked up through a cloudy blur, clawing at the grass. The old man staggered across the haze of his vision, a glint of iron shining in one hand and the air rifle gripped in the other. He saw a glossy, red smear of blood on the butt of the rifle and knew that that was what had hit him; his skull throbbed loudly, warmth spreading and seeping through his hair.

'What are you doing?' Joel moaned as Rudy lurched to the padlocked door of the barn, flicking the glint of iron and jamming it into the lock. Something scratched at the door from inside, grunting and snuffling at the wood.

Rudy paused, his body heaving as though wracked with nerves. Reluctantly he turned his head a few degrees, and Joel saw anger shining wetly in his eyes. 'I hate all this,' he snarled. 'They do this to me every year, you know. Rub their whole Easter schtick in my face. Careless.'

'What?'

'Every year. That's right,' he said mockingly, 'cart all your kids over to *my* farm, throw 'em in *my* pond, disturb all the nature under *my* fuckin nose, just cause *your* fuckin Jesus decided to get out of his cave, or… whatever. Fuckin nuns.'

Joel opened his mouth to say something but an explosion of pain rocked his head back and he winced in the sunlight. Behind the locked door, the creature was clawing madly at the knotted wood.

'And *you*,' Rudy spat, looking back at him. 'Getting in my way.'

Joel shook his head. 'I don't—'

'Fuckin *Easter*. I've had enough, kid.' He began to twist the key in the padlock. 'I. Have. Had… *Enough*.'

'What the hell happened to you?' Joel said, trying to claw his way up onto his knees. Groggy, he shook his head and his brains seemed to rattle. His vision was slowly clearing, but the dull pain at the back of his skull had not begun to fade. 'Why do you hate it so much? What the hell are you *doing*?'

Rudy sighed. Twisted the lock back. Turned, and said, 'She left me at Easter, you know.'

'Your wife?' Joel frowned.

'Maggie? No, my Maggie died in the winter. Cancer bubbled up her throat and took her two weeks before Christmas.'

'So who, then?' Joel said, heaving himself to his feet and clamping a hand down on the bloody mess at the back of his head. Blood seeped through his fingers. His cap lay in the grass, splashed with red.

'My sister,' Rudy said. 'Lizzie. She was a rebel, y'see, not like me. I did my work, got on like Daddy said, never asked no questions. I was ready to stay on this farm my whole life, but Lizzie… she left us when I were a right youngun, didn't she? Easter Day, sun shining bright as it is now, and she just… fucked off and left us. Had other ideas. Met a fella. He promised her everything, as I understand it, and she took him on his word and pissed off with'm.'

'That's why you hate today? That's why you've got this… *thing* in the barn?'

The locked doors shuddered as the creature pounded on them from inside. 'No, I'll tell you why I really hate today,' Rudy said through gritted teeth. 'Ain't cause Lizzie ran away. No. It's cause I *found* her again.'

'Isn't that a good—'

'I found her, after years of lookin, working out of a London brothel without a penny to her name. Her boyfriend had been pimping her out for years – ever since she left, so far as I can tell. She'd had three kids by the time I found her, none of them his. Lost one of them. I reckon he beat the others. And she let him.'

'Rudy, I'm sorry…'

'And the worst part was that she told me she was happier there than she'd ever have been if she hadn't run away. She was twenty-three when I found her, kid. Ten years after she left. Pumped full of heroin and Christ knows what else. All bruised up from where her man had beat her silly. And she told me she didn't regret a thing. Now, I ain't got a thing against that sort of work, you understand… but she was thirteen when he took her, Joel. Thirteen. She ain't ever had a chance to know a different life than that, and she thought he'd given her the world he promised.'

Joel swallowed. Rudy was crying, he realised, thin gelatinous strings running from his eyes like glue.

'Fuckin Easter. And every year these fuckin nuns come down here and remind me what a shit-awful day it is, with their little brats running round screamin and yellin, soiling my pond with their filthy… it ain't no good, see.

'But I'm gonna make sure I'm never disturbed again,' Rudy said quietly. His hand returned to the key in the padlock, and he begun to twist it. 'I don't know where this thing came from, kid, I don't truly know what it is… but it listens t'me, and I'm gonna make 'em all see just what a god-fucked day this is.'

The creature in the barn was clawing and barking at

the door now, and Joel had to shout over the noise. 'You can't do this, Rudy!' he called, looking desperately around for the pitchfork he'd dropped. 'They're just kids!'

'I don't care,' Rudy growled, and he unlocked the door and swung it open.

25

The beast exploded out of the door before it had fully opened, its maw a sloppy mess of spittle and blood, teeth an awful yellow in a whiskered, twitching snout. Its eyes flashed with hunger and it swept toward Joel, splaying its claws. The darkness from within the barn rode its back like a shadowy kind of cloak and its long, ragged ears pressed down against its skull, big wet nostrils flaring.

'No,' Rudy called, swinging the air rifle in the creature's direction, 'not him.'

The thing turned its enormous rabbit-like head toward Rudy, the thick fur of its chest shivering as it breathed rapid shallow breaths. It towered over the boy, a shredded half-tonne of striated muscle and leathery skin, its thick claws spread like mechanical pincers, the weird insectile segments of its torso and legs shining black beneath layers of knotted, blood-matted hair.

'Not him,' Rudy said again, quietly, and jabbed the rifle in the direction of the pond. The sounds of laughter and splashing carried gently toward the barn. '*Them.*'

The creature seemed to grin, its thin black lips stretching back past its pointed teeth. Its ears twitched, then sprung up, batting at imaginary flies around its head. Its eyes flashed darkly and it gave Joel one last hateful look before leaping over him and wheeling toward the distant tree line.

'You monster!' Joel yelled, lurching up as the creature bounded away, clearing the fence into the sheep's field in a single step. It was a streak of darkness, strings of blood and saliva swinging from its face as it punched all four paws into the ground and sprung away. Whirling on the spot, Joel spied the pitchfork in the grass and bent down for it, grabbing it awkwardly and turning back.

Rudy had turned the air rifle on him, now. 'Don't do anything stupid, kid,' he snarled.

'I have to stop it,' Joel spat, brandishing the pitchfork in both hands as if to stab the old man in the stomach. The points glinted in the sunlight as the pounding footsteps of the gigantic rabbit-creature faded to nothing. 'It's going to kill them, Rudy.

They're *kids*.'

Rudy laughed bitterly, glancing down at the pitchfork, the sharp prongs of its head just a single jab away from puncturing his lungs. His grip tightened on the air rifle. 'What, are you gonna try and kill me, are you?'

Joel said nothing. He glanced briefly in the direction of the pond, across the sheep- and wheatfields; the beast had vanished.

'You wouldn't,' Rudy hissed, smiling thinly.

Joel hesitated. He could imagine the tines of the pitchfork punching into Rudy's gut, just beneath his ribs, could imagine twisting into the meat of the old man's body as blood sprayed the grass. He could almost *feel* it. 'No,' he said eventually, lowering the pitchfork. 'I wouldn't.'

'Good boy,' Rudy said, his stance becoming more relaxed. 'Now, if you'll just—'

Joel swung the pitchfork. The speared metal head of the thing crashed into Rudy's skull with a *tong!* and the old man crumpled to the floor, eyes bulging as his head snapped ninety degrees to the side. Winded, he swayed on his knees and collapsed, gasping for air.

'I'm sorry about your sister,' Joel said, squinting toward the trees in the distance. 'But I can't let you do this.'

He turned and ran, following the creature's massive pawprints into the next field.

26

Daylight smashed the surface of the water as glassy shards sprayed the reeds, dampening thick patches of earth and washing the stubble of the cropped field. The banner hung near the pond's edge was smeared with streaks of bright red where a brief overnight spell of rain had spoiled the paint; beneath it, Mother Brunheldt stood in a near-permanent state of applause, clapping her hands politely as the swimmers dashed back and forth across the water.

Around the pond, the St. Adjutor's staff and parents stood in summer dresses and floral print, many of them supervising a small group of children who sat on haybales erected in a horseshoe-shape where the reeds were lower. Those who had already swum shivered in the breeze, wrapped in soaked towels and scratching at the bright red swimming caps on their heads. In the water, a race abruptly finished and the winner, a lithe young boy with bright pink goggles, pumped up his arms in celebration. There was more applause, then a spell of gentle laughter as the children in the pond splashed each other in commiseration. Baskets of chocolate-egg prizes lay hidden in the reeds. Separating her hands for a moment, Mother Brunheldt grabbed a chunky microphone and raised it to her mouth.

'What a brilliant finish there,' she squawked through the whining megaphone. 'And now for the big one – just a moment while the kids get ready—'

Where a pregnant silence might have hung in the air, there was instead a great splashing and chattering as the kids in the pond scrambled out, flopping awkwardly onto the banks, and half a dozen more slipped into the water.

'Perfect,' Brunheldt's voice crackled, 'now, it's the moment you've all been waiting for!'

On the bank, Sisters Emmanuel and Paton helped the kids into their towels and ushered them to the nearest haybale. A hush fell over the small crowd; half of the school was there, sitting and standing among the bales with their eyes on the pond. With her free hand, Mother Brunheldt fumbled a bright glinting medal from her robes.

'For the final race,' she declared, 'I would like you

to complete *ten* lengths of the *Jesus shitting Christ—*'

Sister Emmanuel screamed as she followed Brunheldt's gaze. Another of the nuns turned her head in the same direction and her eyes widened as she saw what the others were looking at. 'The kids!' she shrieked, clamping a hand over her mouth. 'Get the kids out of here!'

'You *monster!*' Brunheldt yelled through the megaphone, the squawking explosion of her voice crackling across the field.

Joel staggered forward, the pitchfork gripped tight in both hands. Blood streamed down the back of his neck and smeared his cheek, and a thick glossy stripe of it decorated one of the pitchfork's speared points. He opened his mouth to protest, but they were all looking at him now, dozens of pairs of eyes fixed on the sharpened weapon in his hands. Deciding to ignore the sudden eruption of chaos, he looked around, head snapping left and right…

Nothing. The creature was nowhere to be seen.

'Where are you?' he yelled, stumbling forward. His gaze lifted, past the pond and into the tree line behind Mother Brunheldt. His eyes snapped from tree to tree as he looked into the shadows of the forest, waiting for something to move. 'It's not here,' he murmured, 'there's nothing here…'

Spangles of light danced on the pond's surface as one of the nuns dived in, scooping a flailing child onto the bank and screaming for help. Some of the kids had scattered but most stared at Joel with a dumbfounded blankness.

Mother Brunheldt's eyes were on fire.

'*YOU GET AWAY FROM MY KIDS!*' she yelled, throwing the megaphone into the reeds and marching forward. At the edge of the pond she raised a shaking finger and waggled it in his direction. 'You psychotic little *turd*! You get away right—'

There was a sudden, heavy *crack* from the woods behind her. Joel's eyes flitted toward the sound and his breath stalled in his throat.

Slowly, Mother Brunheldt turned her head.

The beast exploded from the trees, a rapture of blood-soaked fur and shining black claws. Its ears were pinned back and they twitched as it swung its head left and right, mouth yawing open in its snout, teeth flecked with blood and spit. Its eyes flashed dangerously and it lumbered forward, paws slamming heavily into the dirt.

A moment's silence, and then one of the nuns said, softly, '*Aww.*'

Joel frowned, gaping across the pond at the creature. All around him, the kids were chattering quietly. Nobody was running or screaming; some pointed and giggled.

'It's the Easter Bunny!' one younger child hissed excitedly.

Two of the nuns shared a look. 'Did we pay for this?' one of them whispered.

'Must've,' the other shrugged.

'It's dangerous!' Joel yelled, surging forward suddenly. The creature smiled, stalking around the edge of the pond, eyes laser-focused on him. It flexed its claws and its knuckles clicked awfully. 'Get away from it!'

'Oh, hush,' Sister Paton scowled. 'You're spoiling it for the kids.'

'Aww, look!' a young girl said happily. 'Look at its fluffy little tail!'

Joel blinked, incredulous. 'It's not the Easter Bunny,' he snapped, 'it's—'

'Oh, shut it!' Sister Emmanuel said, shaking her head. She stepped away from the pond, offering her hand to the creature. 'My goodness, look at the detail on the suit!'

They thought it was some kind of mascot, Joel realised. The kids were dumbstruck, enthralled by the sight of the thing, and he supposed they were too naïve to understand what they were looking at – but the sisters had taken to it as well, somehow.

'Oh, this is *joyous*!' Sister Emmanuel squeaked, and she laid a hand on the thing's furry chest. Turning her head, she grinned cheerfully in Mother Brunheldt's direction. 'Oh, happy, happy Easter—'

The creature snapped forward suddenly and

clamped its jaws over Emmanuel's head, ripping it back and severing her neck immediately. Blood sprayed her dress and the nearby kids as her body staggered back a step, bone and cartilage shining as they poked up through the viscera of her neck. Matted hair and flesh slopped in the creature's mouth as it tipped back its head and chewed, bones crunching between its teeth.

Sister Emmanuel's headless body took another step, then crumpled to its knees. It swayed for a minute, a thick wall of red gloop rushing down its front, then it toppled into the pond with a splash. Red mist coiled in the water and spread around her.

The creature spat out bone and reached up to wipe its snout with one bony, clawed hand. Grinning with a mouthful of blood and hair, it looked around.

Now they started to scream.

27

Kids spilled away from the pond in a haphazard mess of bodies as the beast surged forward, plunging a fist into the spine of the nearest sister and ripping out a chunk of sloppy viscera. The nun screamed as she fell forward, crimson goop spraying from the ruptured cavern of her back. Stamping on her convulsing body as it stepped closer to the pond, the rabbit-thing looked around for its next target, hunger burning bright red in its eyes.

Joel was frozen to the spot, stunned to petrification by the sudden explosion of violence. He could do nothing but blink as the creature leapt onto the chest of another nun and punched her body into the reeds, latching onto her neck with its powerful jaws and shredding meat and gore from her. Gripping both sides of her head with its claws, it twisted and a dull, blunt *crack* echoed across the pond, somehow drowning out all the screaming chaos around them.

There was a shriek from across the pond and the rabbit-thing looked up, ears pinned back. Grinning, its eyes locked onto Mother Brunheldt and it sprung off the body in the reeds, landing in the water with a great splash and disappearing under the surface. Joel looked up and saw that Brunheldt had her arms spread wide, a gaggle of kids sheltering behind her. She wasn't the one who'd screamed – her face was determinedly protective and bewilderingly unafraid – but the sound had drawn the creature toward her. She glanced across the pond at Joel and he saw the fear in her eyes, buried deep beneath that mask of stony stillness but there nonetheless. She was trying to protect them, he thought, that was all. And it was going to kill her.

Joel balked as the creature reared up from the pond in a great cascade of dirty water, its fur soaked and pressed to its awful insect-like skin, a sheen of clotted blood clinging to its body. It spread its claws wide and roared, a great explosion of sound from deep within its stomach. Brunheldt backed away, pushing the kids back, opening her mouth to finally scream in defiance—

'Leave her alone!' Joel yelled, his throat ripped to pieces by the surprising, savage desperation of the cry. 'Come get me, *fucker*!'

The rabbit-thing turned its head, eyes flashing brightly.

'That's it,' Joel whispered, bracing the pitchfork as his eyes flitted between Brunheldt and the bunny. He watched carefully as she ushered the kids away, taking the opportunity to scramble back from the creature. Then it turned its body fully, flexing its claws, every joint in its beastly frame clicking as it crouched down on its heels, preparing to pounce. 'Come on, then, fucking come on…'

The creature leapt, springing into the reeds and bounding around the pond, punching all four paws into the ground like an enraged bull as it pounced at him. Joel backed up quickly, getting as far from the nearest kids as he could, looking all around for a gap, for somewhere to run. The creature sprung toward him and he acted on instinct, thrusting the pitchfork forward.

'Yaaagh!' he yelled as he jabbed the spikes into the creature's stomach. There was a papery shredding sound as the weapon pierced the beast's chitinous flesh and sunk wetly into muscle. Joel twisted, cringing as thin, grey blood sprayed his face.

The creature yowled, grabbing the shaft of the pitchfork with one clawed fist and wrenching it out of Joel's grip. The boy's eyes widened as the creature drew the fork easily from its own body, a gushing spray of gunky fluid jetting into the reeds.

It tossed the pitchfork into the pond and looked

down at Joel, its eyes hot with anger.

'Shit.'

There was a shrill whistling sound as the creature raked the air with its claws, swinging wildly as it lurched toward him. Rudy had stopped it from killing him before but now Rudy wasn't here; now there was nothing between him and the thing and it wouldn't stop, not unless he managed to kill it first…

Joel ducked under the creature's snapping jaws, a whiff of hot breath blooming over his face. He rolled under a swinging set of claws and lurched into an awkward run, staggering past the pond, the stubble of the field crunching beneath his feet.

'Fuck!' he yelled as claws raked his back and a sweeping burst of heat spread up his spine. He doubled over, narrowly avoiding a second swipe for his head, kept running, heart pounding, legs aching already. Adrenaline pumped hotly through his blood and he could hear the kids' screams fading, knew that even if it got him, at least he had earned them all a few seconds' headstart. He hoped Brunheldt would have the sense to get them into the vans and get them the hell out of here. Perhaps he could stay out of the creature's claws long enough for the police to get here, or someone who could—

Something hard smacked his back and shattered. He yelped, dipping to one side and chancing a look over his shoulder. A mess of bright pink eggshell lay in a puddle of goop in the earth. Another wet *crack* and something smashed his shoulder. Chunks of shell stuck to his jacket and he batted at the mess, crying out as something moved in the gluey knot of gunk around his hand. Thin, spidery legs rattled out of the broken shell and clamped over his fingers, the tiny creature latching onto him. He smacked the back of the insect-like thing and scooped it off him, flinging it into the dirt.

The rabbit-thing roared in his ear and he realised he'd stopped running. Whirling around he yelled out, insane images flashing through his mind. *Shark*, he thought suddenly and his fist launched itself forward before he could stop it, landing squarely with a *thomp* in the creature's nose. It blinked, staggered back, and he took his chance to keep running. Ducking a swinging claw he looked up and saw the haystack in the distance, glittering in the sunlight, still wet with gasoline.

Now there was an idea.

'Chase me,' he whispered, and he sprinted forward. Behind him the creature hurled another egg and it struck his calf, smashing to pieces instantly. The tiny infant thing within went into attack mode the second it hatched, biting into the meat of his leg. Joel screamed and continued, more eggs hitting his back and legs, more insect-like things sprawling out of them and rattling over his body. Gaining on the haystack, he fumbled in his pocket for the lighter and glanced back.

Behind him, the rabbit-thing grinned madly, spreading its claws as its eyes lit up. Its gaze locked on Joel and it opened its maw wide – wider, dislocating like a snake's – and Joel balked as a mess of hard, black spines sprung out of its throat, peeling back the lips to reveal a set of shining, bloody mandibles.

An awful clicking roar erupted from its neck and it launched itself at him.

28

Joel yelped as the creature lunged forward, ducking a swinging limb and lashing out at another of the gunk-covered spider-babies that had latched onto the lapel of his jacket. In the blurred spike of movement that followed he saw a gaping slash across the beast's midsection, red and grey swirled into the gore that drizzled from it; where the pitchfork had pierced the thing's flesh, it had opened a wide cavern in its belly, and inside Joel saw flashes of colour – red, yellow, pink, and that sickening pastel blue – eggs swilling about inside a meaty sac of skin that Joel could only assume was some kind of awful womb.

All the while it had been chasing him, the rabbit-thing had been dipping its great clawed hands into the wound that Joel had ripped from its belly and flinging its unborn spawn at him.

Jesus fucking Christ.

'Get back!' Joel yelled as he staggered backward, crashing into the lowest level of the pyramid-shaped haystack behind him. His heel slipped awkwardly and he glanced down, saw that the ground was still shining and wet with gasoline. His eyes flitted up again as the rabbit-thing bore down on him, claws crashing together as he ducked his head and rolled out of the way. Fluid streaked his back and he stumbled to his feet, fumbling in his jeans for the lighter.

The creature dug a hand into its stomach and ripped the skin loose, an awful papery clicking accompanying the sound of shredding flesh. A jumble of multicoloured eggs fell out of the pouch of its torso and shattered on the ground, a cacophony of piercing shrieks rising from the mess as half a dozen spider-like embryos wriggled free of their gelatinous, gunk-grey casing. Spiny legs poked through sheer membranes and tiny jaws snapped hungrily as they skittered forward.

Joel lunged forward, grasping the lighter tight in his hand and flicking it open. He ploughed his body toward the very bottom of the haystack, reaching out as he desperately flicked the wheel—

Hot pain smashed his face as a cluster of tiny legs pierced his cheek. The spawn-thing swung from his face as he tipped his head back, punching the rattling creature off of his cheek and into the grass. Another slammed into the back of his neck and dug its claws in and he cried out, looking all around for the enormous rabbit-monster that had spawned them…

Nothing. It had disappeared and left him with the tiny fuckers.

'Shit,' he said, lunging for the haystack and digging in with both hands. 'Shit, shit, shit…'

He climbed frantically, ignoring the pain in his neck as the little insect-creature's miniature teeth pierced skin. Another clung to his ankle, trying to bite through his shoe, and a pair hung on to his jacket with their pincers, swinging madly as he stumbled awkwardly onto the first level. He hauled himself up the next haybale and took a moment to catch his breath. This wouldn't work, not if the creature was gone, not if it had realised what he was planning and run away.

He grabbed the top haybale with both hands and started to heave himself up. Nearly there, he thought, panting hard, his heart pounding, nearly—

The haystack shuddered as a gigantic shadow loomed over him, the rabbit-thing's frame blotting out all the sunlight as it spread its claws and surged forward. Joel lost his grip and stumbled, rolling his ankle as he was knocked halfway down the haystack. Immediately the creature sprung over the top of the pyramid and landed in the hay before him, its giant, long feet punching into the bale and spraying yellow stubble into the wind.

The hay stunk of gasoline and Joel realised he had one chance left. Now, he thought, *do it now*.

He fumbled, brought up the lighter, looked up into the shining hungry eyes of the creature as he flipped the wheel to ignite it. A tiny flame shot up from the wick and he plunged his hand down, down into the gasoline-soaked hay.

The lighter never made it.

Joel yowled as the creature's head surged forward, leathery ears flapping backward as it opened its jaws wide and clamped them around his wrist. In less than a second it had torn through his arm with a dreadful, wet *crunch* and he felt a sudden weightlessness as his fist disappeared into the creature's throat, lighter and all. There was a ripping sound as the rabbit-thing tore its head back, a carnival of viscera spraying the haystack as tiny chunks of bone flew back on the wind.

Joel screamed. But he had no time to try and stem the blood pumping freely from the stump of his arm, or lament the loss of the only hope he'd had of stopping the creature; before he could fully react it had grabbed him by the shoulders and dragged him onto his feet, snarling and spitting in his face. Joel smelled death on its tongue and his eyes went wide, heart skipping the next dozen beats as it launched into overdrive.

The rabbit-thing spun him round and launched a foot into his spine, sending him flying off the haystack into the dirt beneath. Joel threw up as he fell, his ears pounding. With the taste of bile in his mouth he sprawled in the earth at the bottom of the haystack. He thought his back might be broken. Rolling onto it he looked up and howled in agony.

The rabbit-thing leered down at him from its place at the top of the pyramid, claws and mouth smeared with his gore.

'Ohh,' Joel groaned, reaching with one shaking hand for the shredded stump of the other.

As he moved, his good hand brushed against something in his jacket pocket. A small, slim box.

Grimly, he smiled.

'Got you,' he whispered, reaching into his pocket and gently sliding the matchbox open. Around him, tiny spider-creatures scuttled and danced through the gasoline-soaked earth, their shells sprayed with blood. Above him the rabbit-thing roared, its throat clicking as it let loose a triumphant bellow.

Plucking a single match from the box, Joel withdrew the whole thing from his pocket and tossed it into the earth. Looking up one last time, he closed his eyes and one-handedly struck the match against the lighting paper.

Whoomph.

29

When he woke up there was pain.

Bright white lights seared his vision, foggy and swimming around him. His entire right arm stung, like the world's biggest bee had left its stinger in his wrist and the whole thing was infected. His chest and back ached like mad, his bones turned to mush inside him. His skin tingled. There was something thick and suffocating laid across his chest.

A bright flare of amber as the haystack went up, flames surging through its heart and exploding over every flake of yellow.

His eyes widened in panic, then winced them shut again as the burning bright light grew immediately unbearable. 'Shit,' he whispered, his voice hoarse, throat painful and raw. 'Am I…'

The rattling screech of the creature as its leg sunk into the crumbling pile, claws sprawling. Thick tongues of fire lashing its back, its chest, ripping their way up its throat—

'I'm dead,' Joel rasped. 'Fuck.'

'Not quite,' came a familiar voice from somewhere above him. 'But you might be if you keep on with language like that around me.'

Joel's eyes snapped open. Pain shot through his spine as he leant forward to look in the direction of the voice.

'Careful, there,' Mother Brunheldt said softly, her figure a faint black shape in the swimming mess of his vision. 'I don't think you're quite at the "sitting up" stage, Joel.'

Sinking back into the thin mattress, Joel registered a faint beeping from somewhere in the room. Closed his eyes again. 'Hospital,' he muttered.

'Yes.'

'My hand—'

'Don't think about it.'

'I can *feel* it.'

'No, Joel, you can't. But that's something you're going to have to get used to.'

He heard muffled conversation in the corridor. Wearily, he blinked his eyes open again and looked up at the ceiling. 'The kids?'

'All safe. Thanks to you,' Brunheldt said, and

suddenly Joel felt a hand on his arm. She squeezed gently, and there was a thin smile in her voice: 'You saved their lives, Joel.'

'Rudy…' Joel moaned, memories splitting his head open.

'Gone.'

'The eggs—'

'We found as many as we could. They're damn *hard* to find, you know.'

Joel couldn't help but laugh weakly at the mental image of Brunheldt and her sisters conducting an Easter egg hunt around the farm. The laugh faded, and he turned his head to look at her. She was sat in her habit in a white plastic chair beside the bed, a thick red book folded in her lap. She must have been waiting for him to wake up.

'Something on your mind?' she said softly.

Joel swallowed. His arm twitched with the memory of his fingers. He shook his head.

'Tell me.'

'The lighter…' Joel said. 'My dad's lighter. I thought it was going to work. But it… I can't help thinking… it let me down, right at the end. Right when I needed it the most. It… disappeared. Just like he did.'

Mother Brunheldt leaned forward, and her face was more serious than he'd ever seen it. But there was a kindness in her eyes that reminded him of home. Smiling weakly, Brunheldt opened her mouth, closed it, and tried again. 'Joel, I can't begin to imagine how difficult it was for you when your father did what he did. But then – and now, with this, with those matches – it was down to *you* to survive, to keep going, to find faith in your own resourcefulness and find a way out of a terrible situation, and do you know what? Both times, *you* did it.'

Joel nodded.

'Remember this, Joel. Your parents contributed to who you are. Your dad… even your mum. If not for all the awful things you'd experienced, you wouldn't *be* who you are. But *contribution* isn't *creation*. You took all those things they offered you, and you *made* yourself. Do you understand?'

He didn't, not fully, but he nodded all the same.

'You made it out of this, because you are all the things that you're made of. And if your father was still around, Joel, I know he'd be proud of you. Don't you think?'

Joel blinked. Eyes heavy, he slurred, 'I wonder what… those eggies would have tasted like… scrambled.'

Mother Brunheldt cocked an eyebrow. 'Are you a little high on painkillers?'

Joel shrugged and another bolt of black pain seared his spine. 'Can I have more?'

Brunheldt laughed gently, squeezing his arm again. 'Sleep for a while,' she said, 'and if you want to talk more about this when you wake up, then I'll be around.'

She paused.

'You fancy coming back to school when you're better?'

Joel swallowed guiltily.

'Think about it,' she smiled, getting up to leave the room. Before she turned from him she leant toward a small bedside cabinet and gently laid something on top. 'I'll see you soon, Joel.'

He watched her leave through a haze of white and burning bright lights. When she'd gone, he cried for a little while. And when a little of that haze had faded, he tilted up his eyes to look toward the bedside cabinet, and he saw his lighter.

His dad's lighter.

It was entirely mangled, and scorched all along one edge, but Brunheldt had polished it lovingly for him.

Weeping hotly as an overwhelming surge of emotion coursed up his throat, Joel reached for the lighter with his good hand and clutched it tight.

With the smell of burning in his nostrils, he cried himself almost happily to sleep.

Epilogue

Moonlight filtered through the treetop canopy, throwing spangles of blue and white into a foliage of dead and broken things. An eerie stillness clung to the trees, the absence of birdsong amplified into a deafening smack of silence that echoed impossibly.

In the shadow of a tall, grey ash, a single egg lay abandoned in the leaves. Its shell was a strange orange colour, mottled and lumpen, dappled grey by the moonlight.

It pulsed.

A moment or two passed, then the egg wobbled.

A thin, splintery crack danced suddenly down its shell, a webbing of graphite-grey spreading across its surface—

And an enormous, black shape lurched forward and

snatched it from the ground, chewing hungrily and tossing the broken pieces of shell down its throat.

A beat of silence.

The shadows swelled as the creature stood from its crouching position in the foliage, unfolding from the dark as though it was an extension of the night itself. Bright, white eyes flared in the shadows and enormous claws spread wide as it stepped out of the shade of the ash tree, reaching up to wipe a smear of eggshell from its maw.

It sniffed the air and turned its head toward a blinking, distant light.

Crumpling onto all fours, the creature slunk through the trees, sharp ears pinned back against its head. Its back was driven through with shivering, black spines, and out of its jaws a long, thick tongue snaked, segmented and spiked. A snake-like tail darted between its legs.

The creature smiled as it reached the edge of the forest, white teeth flashing in the moonlight. Standing again on its hind legs, it rolled its enormous head from side to side and howled at the distant farmhouse, the mournful wail echoing off the surface of a nearby pond and carrying on the wind.

They had killed its mate.

They would suffer for that.

www.ingramcontent.com/pod-product-compliance
Lightning Source LLC
Chambersburg PA
CBHW061924220726
48287CB00018B/860